OOPS! I SUMMONED A LIDERC

Witches Love Monsters

REGINE ABEL

COVER DESIGN BY
Regine Abel

ILLUSTRATIONS BY
Morgan
Hojolabor
Vvevelur

Copyright © 2025

CONTENTS

OOPS! I SUMMONED A LIDERC

Crack an egg, hatch a demon!

When Coral goes to pick up the remaining belongings her obnoxious ex-roommate Angelique left in their old flat, she inadvertently starts the mother of all shitstorms. How was Coral to know that she'd brought back Vazul—an insanely hot sex demon, with a sharp tongue and wicked wits? She should cast him out, but the thought of parting ways with her irreverent demon is unbearable.

With Angelique hellbent on reclaiming what she deems hers, should Coral protect Vazul from the nefarious plans that wicked witch has in store for him, or should she seize the opportunity to run?

DEDICATION

To those who show kindness for its own sake and not in the hopes of being praised or compensated for it. You are seen far more than you realize. A good soul is like a beacon shining brightly, bringing happiness, and uplifting all who get to bask in your aura. When you least expect it, but need it the most, the same beautiful light will shine right back on you.

Do not let those who seek to steal and appropriate your light make you stray from your path. Darkness cannot encroach on our lives unless we choose to let it in.

To those who embrace their inner demons.

CHAPTER 1
CORAL

No words could express the depth of the annoyance I felt as I stared at the pile of junk I had to haul back. Dear, sweet, and extremely obnoxious Angelique always had to find a way to be a thorn in my side.

When I left the apartment I had been sharing with her and Sophia three months ago, I thought I was done with her nonsense. Granted, I bailed out before the end of our lease, but I paid my remaining share upfront so they couldn't claim I screwed them over somehow. It had been an amicable split. As I left so early on, my two ex-roommates agreed that they would tackle the final cleaning before their departure.

Sophia did her part, as expected. But miss diva Angelique had to leave some other crap behind. And the landlady wasn't having it. With Sophia being out of town for a wedding, and Angie conveniently being stuck in some other engagement also out of town, it all fell back on me. It didn't matter that she only had four bags and a couple additional knickknacks. None of this should be my problem anymore. But as I didn't want to be stuck paying cleaning penalties since my name remained on the lease, here I was sacrificing my time and playing mover.

Mrs. Hopkins cleared her throat with less-than-subtle impatience. I much preferred dealing with the superintendent than with this dragon of a landlady. To be fair, she wasn't rude or mean per se. She just made you immediately stand up straight as if under military review.

Tall and skinny, the older woman in her late fifties stared at me with her obsidian eyes assessing me over narrow glasses. Her long black hair was held tightly into the most perfect bun. You'd think every single strand was too scared to misbehave. She didn't even need gel to keep them in place. She always wore black suits with the appropriate knee length skirt, a pristine white shirt beneath the vest, and black high heels so polished you could see your reflection in them. You'd never catch her without makeup on, flawlessly applied, which enhanced her features in a natural and elegant fashion.

Every time I stood in her presence, I felt like an unruly child about to be scolded by the head mistress of a strict reform school for girls.

Not wanting to try her patience longer than necessary, I reached for the big bags she'd thankfully prepacked for me. My body leaning in a way to hide what I was doing, I cast a discreet strength spell on myself. I should have done it before I entered the apartment but never expected there would be this much stuff left. Although most people believed magic to be an old wives' tale, it wasn't. However, you didn't go around advertising that we were active in the craft. And even less so when you were just a dabbler like me.

First, I picked up the fancy ermine cloak sitting on top of the bags and stuffed it under my left arm. Then, I grabbed two bags in each hand. The wretched things were overflowing. How she managed to zip them shut could qualify as witchcraft in and of itself.

"Off I go and sorry for the inconvenience," I told Mrs. Hopkins with a stiff smile.

She gave me the strangest look, my senses going into high alert when the most subtle smirk quirked the corner of her thin lips.

"Not so fast, Coral. You forgot one thing," she said in that overly polite tone receptionists sometimes gave you.

I blinked, confused as to what she was referring to, then glanced at the floor around the narrow entrance for any signs of what I might have missed. She snapped her fingers, making me jerk my head up.

"Not down there but up here," she said, pointing an elegantly manicured index finger at the console propped against the left wall.

She reached for an egg-shaped black stone sitting atop it.

"What is that?" I asked, confused.

"Another of Angelique's belongings," Mrs. Hopkins said with a blasé tone and a dismissive shrug.

"That's trash!" I exclaimed disbelievingly. "Who cares about a rock? And anyway, you can see that I have no room to carry this."

"Tut, tut," she replied with a mulish expression. "Everything is to be removed as I am not getting sued for missing property."

"But—"

Before I could finish whatever I intended to say, Mrs. Hopkins stuffed the rock under my armpit, right above the ermine.

"See? All set!" she said in an overly smug tone that made me want to kick her. "Now off you go!"

Annoyed to no end, I muttered something under my breath, gave her a stiff nod, and turned around to leave.

"Just so you know, Miss Reef, the most insignificant objects are often the most valuable," she said in a mysterious tone.

Ya, that was me, Coral Reef. My parents were the hipster type who thought of themselves as witty and the most hilarious of comedians. Instead, they just stockpiled the Darwin Awards of

Cringe. Sadly for me, I'd been born during the craze where parents were trying too hard to be overly clever with baby names. I actually liked my first name. It was the combo with my surname I could have lived without. But hey, it beat funky given names like Tu Morrow, Angel Face, and Skibidi like some unfortunate souls I met got 'blessed' with. Still, I loved my parents with all their quirks.

"What?" I asked, confused as I glanced over my shoulder at her.

She gave me that mysterious look again. But this time, the intensity of her dark gaze unsettled me.

"You'll see. But you should hurry before your cab leaves," she said with an almost taunting smile.

"Oh fuck!" I muttered and immediately flinched. "Sorry!"

She didn't say a word but only stared at me. I mumbled another apology before hurrying out. I hated being this loaded, but my strength spell was working its magic, making the otherwise heavy bags feel like nothing. I rushed to the elevator only to see the cabin flying down.

I stopped dead in my tracks, threw my head back, and closed my eyes as I groaned loudly. As much as I had loved living in this antique building—which was classified as historical—I always had mixed feelings about the old school wooden elevator. It stood out with its ornate detailing and glass windows that allowed you to look around the building as you climbed up and down. It also possessed a retractable metal grid that served as a safety door, which had to be closed on every floor in order for the cabin to move. Sadly, it was as beautiful as it was slow.

As I couldn't risk waiting forever for it to come back— assuming a different floor hadn't called it before me—I settled for the stairs. Once again, I patted myself on the back for that strength spell. Without it, I'd be freaking out. It didn't make my legs any less wobbly by the time I reached the lobby from the fifth floor.

As I hurried towards the entrance, I inwardly uttered a string of unladylike curses when I found the elevator empty and the cage door open. If I had still been upstairs, I'd be waiting for that lift until the cows came home as it would never move until that door was closed. A part of me almost felt guilty for not going to close it for whoever else might need it. However, not only was this no longer my problem, but I had a cab to catch.

I half jogged out of the building only for my heart to sink when the spot where my cab had been waiting stood empty. Panicked, I jerked my head in both directions of the street only to see the rear end of my cab with its blinkers on as it was leaving without me.

"Are you fucking kidding me?!" I exclaimed, utterly pissed off.

I hadn't been gone so long that it couldn't have waited. Granted, time was money, and with the amount of business the drivers got, it paid more for them to do runs than to sit idling while waiting for a customer.

I glared up at the window of my old apartment only to find Mrs. Hopkins staring down at me. Even from a distance, I could see the weirdest smirk on her face. If I didn't know better—or at least hoped better—I would assume she had sent my cab away. But how would that benefit her?

Defeated, I put the two bags in my right hand on the ground, whipped out my phone, and dialed with one hand to call another cab. As I feared, they informed me of the excessively high volume of requests which meant it would be close to forty minutes or more before they could have someone pick me up.

The depth of rage that burned in my guts couldn't be put into words. For one very serious moment, I considered just trashing all Angelique's belongings. I wasn't her fucking maid or errand girl. But being my dumb people pleaser self, I sucked it up again and just made my way to the nearest bus station. It truly felt like a conspiracy theory.

I had my own car, which conveniently happened to be at the garage getting an oil change and tuning. Had they warned me sooner that this needed to be handled today, I would have postponed the maintenance. But nope, Mrs. Hopkins called me not even an hour after I dropped off the car to tell me to come fetch everything since the others couldn't. Otherwise, we'd all face a fine.

Next time, just pay the fucking fine.

With it being early fall, the weather was already a bit chilly. Thankfully, I didn't have to wait long for the next bus to arrive. However, there was a reason I avoided public transportation as the damn things were always packed here. And today was no exception.

I squeezed my way to the middle of the bus before getting sandwiched by far too many bodies. With so many of them wearing coats or thick sweaters, it didn't take long before I started feeling a bit too hot. I encouraged myself with the thought that it was only a ten-minute ride. If I tried to pretend I was in a sauna instead of a sea of humans, it might be a bit more bearable.

Except a sauna doesn't smell like unwashed armpits and garlic breath.

And a burly dude on the left, all but towering over me, was zealously hammering me with both. It was in situations like this that I berated myself for not pursuing my witchcraft training with more assiduity. I'd give my left tit now for a stench suppression spell.

Just as I was bemoaning my situation, a violent shock suddenly rocked the bus, accompanied by a loud crashing sound. If not for the countless bodies squished together like sardines in the vehicle, I probably would have flown a few meters from the force of the impact. My stomach roiled with that freaky roller coaster feeling as the bus spun around before coming to a brutal stop as it slammed into something else. Sore and dizzy, it took me a moment to regain my bearings between all the screaming, moaning, and pushing as people tried to straighten or avoid getting crushed.

It took a moment before the people closest to the windows were able to communicate to the rest of us what had happened. Some vehicle had crossed a red light, ramming into the bus, sending us into a tailspin. Except we couldn't get off as the front doors were busted in. The back doors were also blocked by the lamp post we'd crashed against, and which had stopped us from spinning farther away. The only positive in this mess was the absence of grievous injuries among the passengers.

To my dismay, it took them over half an hour to pry us out of what quickly started feeling like a freaking oven. The bus was getting hot and suffocating. By the foul smell wafting my way, at least one or two people had sullied themselves in the scare. Added to the 'eau de sweat and garlic' perfume my neighbor graced us with, it made the situation even less tenable.

Sweat was rolling down my back. Worse still, my armpit began to itch. But with the damn stone egg stuck underneath it, I could only try to wiggle in the hope of getting some relief. Then I felt a crack. My eyes nearly popped out of my head as my heart sank. The last thing I needed was for the contents of some rotten black egg to ooze all over Angie's fancy ermine and my clothes in this freaking hellhole.

To my relief, the egg appeared to be intact. But that false alarm was enough to make me stand still.

After an eternity and a day, they finally let us off. The cool air never felt more wonderful. When they directed us to hop into another bus they specifically brought to get the uninjured people on their way, I almost declined. But I couldn't see myself walking the remaining four miles home.

Thankfully, karma apparently decided that I'd had enough for one day, and the rest of the journey home went by undisturbed. I couldn't recall being happier at the sight of my house, other than the day I officially received the keys when I bought it a few months ago. I stepped inside the house and dropped the four bags at the entrance by the console. After carefully removing the egg from under my armpit, I plopped the ermine on top of the bags.

My jaw dropped when I noticed what appeared to be a fissure on the black shell of the egg. Although it had the same shine as a polished stone, the texture truly felt like that of an egg, even though it was far too hard to be one. The crack on it seemed to glow from within, as if it contained red flames. The egg felt unusually hot to the touch, but not as if something was burning inside. Could it simply be the heat of my body from having held it under my armpit for nearly two hours?

I groaned inwardly at the prospect of the hissy fit Angie was bound to throw once she noticed that her property had been damaged. The entitled bitch would likely also demand some form of monetary compensation, even though she absolutely didn't hurt for it.

Once again, I berated myself for bringing this shit on me with my stupid need to save people from their own stupidity and laziness.

Maybe I can just hide it from her.

I seriously contemplated doing just that. Chances were that Angie didn't even remember having that egg rock. The problem was that she eventually would when something related popped up. And then she'd be foaming at the mouth demanding her property be returned forthwith with copious accusations of me being a thief.

Fuck my life. There's simply no winning.

Not wanting to risk damaging the egg further if it fell, I headed into the kitchen and pulled out a large fruit bowl. I placed a thick towel in it and carefully settled the egg in the middle, tucking the towel all around it to make sure it was snug and stable.

Impatient to wash off the stench from the bus and the heat, I hopped into the shower, grateful for the delightful and soothing caress of the water on me. I had just begun lathering some soap all over my body when a loud sound startled me. I gasped, turned off the water, and strained my ear to see if I was hearing something else or if my imagination was playing tricks on me. When the silence continued, I shrugged and resumed my ablutions.

Moments after I began rinsing, I heard another loud crack followed by what sounded like a hiss. This time, I no longer believed I'd imagined it. I quickly rinsed off to avoid slipping and breaking my neck then wrapped a towel around me. Cursing myself for not pushing my magic training further, I grabbed a pair of scissors and carefully opened the door.

"Is anyone there?" I called out, wondering if this was stupid to let them know I was on to them or a good way to scare off any potential intruder.

For a split second, I considered putting some clothes on before I went to investigate. But then I figured I'd much rather run outside bare ass and alive than to get stabbed by a serial killer with one leg halfway stepping into my panties.

As the sound came from downstairs, I didn't want to remain cooped up here on the second floor with no way out. Straining my ears for any suspicious activity, I carefully made my way down the stairs, my long scissors held firmly in my right hand. I never rejoiced more that my floors didn't creak.

My brain immediately registered that the front door was still closed and the bags remained undisturbed by the console. No visible sign of disturbance indicated the presence of an intruder. However, as I reached the landing and glanced to the right towards the kitchen, my heart skipped a beat at the sight of a pulsating reddish glow. I half ran into the kitchen thinking that something was on fire only to stop dead in my tracks when I saw the source of the glow.

Many more cracks had appeared on the surface of the egg visible over the towel wrapped around it. From where I stood, it literally looked as if a heart was beating inside. With a will of their own, my feet carried me to the island upon which the bowl sat. With great care, I pulled the towel away to expose more of the egg. A network of cracks covered its dark surface. And yet, it retained an apparent integrity.

For a reason I would never be able to explain, my stupid brain decided it was a good idea to pick it up. The intense burn I expected never came, even though it appeared filled with lava. It was very warm but in a pleasant way.

What the fuck is hatching out of this?

Angie often collected exotic stuff, but she was too selfish to raise pets. Well, except for her black cat, Merlin, as he was fairly low maintenance. When we were roommates, Sophia and I shouldered the brunt of grooming and feeding the cat. Now, Angie had her cleaning lady do it except for feeding. Everything about Angie focused on acquiring more power and increasing her magic or leverage over others. She had no time for anything that would demand she care for it. So what in the world was this about?

As I was still very much a novice in the arcane world, I didn't know jack shit about the kind of funky critter that could pop out of a black egg.

Unsure as to what to do, I glanced around the room debating where I should put it to hatch. It needed a safe place as I didn't want it to fall from the counter if it couldn't fly. But even as that thought crossed my mind, images of nightmarish creatures took over. What if it was some sort of flying flesh-eating monster that came out and chewed me up? Should I find some sort of cage or containment device to put it in while I call the Council of Witches for help?

Calling Angie would have been the easiest solution, but I had attempted to reach her in vain at least three times this morning since Mrs. Hopkins demanded I come to pick up her stuff. I couldn't tell if she truly was too busy or was deliberately ignoring my calls knowing that I would likely berate her for dumping her shit on me.

Any such musings flew right out of my mind as a loud crack resonated again. My heart nearly jumped out of my chest as the egg violently wiggled in my hands. I screeched and instinctively dropped it in shock.

"No!" I shouted as I watched it plummet to the travertine tiled floor of the kitchen as if in slow motion.

To my dismay, the egg didn't shatter and spill its fiery red goop onto the floor. Instead, countless cracks slithered all over its obsidian surface, and it shuddered violently once, twice... And then the top flew off as a black, clawed hand shot out of the egg. I screamed again and quickly backed away until the wall stopped my retreat. Frozen in fear, I just stood there, wishing for the wall to swallow me whole.

Before me, a humanoid shape sprung out of the broken shell like a genie from its lamp. He quickly took shape as a muscular male with a haunting human face, a long pair of horns poking straight up, glowing red eyes, long wavy black hair, and pointy ears. Except, he wasn't a genie. As his entire body emerged from the egg, so did a long pair of muscular legs. He appeared to slowly float back down onto the floor where he stood in his glorious nudity. His entire skin was the darkest shade of gray, almost charcoal. Beneath it, fiery lightning pulsated as if lava wanted to erupt from him.

Under different circumstances, my gaze would have zeroed in on his massive cock—limp though it currently was—covered in unusual ridges.

A predatory smile stretched his plump lips, giving me a glimpse of perfect white teeth framed by a pair of sharp fangs. He flicked his right hand, and it glowed an angry red. Simultaneously, the scattered fragments of his shell began to sizzle and wither before vanishing in a puff of smoke.

"Hello, Mistress," the demon said in a deep, sensual voice

that had goosebumps erupting all over my body. "So lightly clad. Someone is eager... I approve."

He added those last two words in a purring voice as he began to prowl towards me. That finally snapped me out of my terrified daze. I screeched again and made a mad dash towards the front door.

A discreet swoosh resonated behind me half a beat before a ball of fire flew past me at dizzying speed. At first, I thought the demon had shot a fiery ball at me. But the blazing sphere stopped directly in front of the door before shifting into the dark demon. I tried to stop but lost my footing instead. I slipped and watched my feet go up in front of me as I landed with a loud thud on the hardwood floor. Pain radiated from my right butt cheek, down my leg, and up my lower back. Carried by my momentum, I slid a few extra feet towards him, flashing him with both my butt and cooch on full display.

"Ow!" I whimpered, hurt, humiliated, and terrified.

To my shock, an air of real concern—oddly mixed with disapproval—descended over the demon's face.

"Mistress! Look at what you did to yourself! Where are you running off to?" he asked, lunging towards me.

Before I could even scramble back onto my feet, he picked me up effortlessly, holding me tightly against him as the treacherous towel just fell off. My breath caught in my throat, and I emitted the weirdest gurgling choked sound when he casually rubbed his left hand over my butt cheek while holding me firmly against him with his right arm wrapped around my back.

"What a perfect behind," he mused aloud. "You can't damage it with such reckless behavior."

I screamed again and shoved against his chest to free myself from his embrace. He winced at the shrill sound and looked at me as if I was mentally impaired.

"Put me down!" I shouted.

He immediately released his hold. I gasped, shocked to find

myself falling. My feet landed on the floor at a bad angle. Being a ripe old bitch, gravity pulled me backward. Eyes wide, I instinctively reached forward for something to hold onto. Moving at lightning speed, the demon caught my wrist, steadying me before I crashed again.

I yanked my arm free and stumbled a few steps away from him. The unimpressed look on his face stung something fierce.

"You can't even stand," he said in a disapproving tone.

"I said put me down, not drop me like a freaking potato sack!" I exclaimed, outraged. "So of course, I almost fell again."

I swiftly grabbed the towel on the floor and wrapped it around me as I took a couple more steps back. Although my mind kept telling me to run the hell out of here, the initial terrified panic had subsided. If he wanted to eat me and use my bones as toothpicks, he would have already done so by now. But he immediately complied when I asked him to put me down. So maybe he wasn't all that bad?

He pursed his lips with clear disappointment as he stared at the towel.

"What a pity to obstruct such a nice view," he said in that same disapproving tone.

"What the fuck?!" I whispered incomplete disbelief. "Who are you? And what the hell are you?"

"I am Vazul, and I am your Liderc."

"You're my what, now?" I asked, stunned.

"Your Liderc," he repeated with a frown as if wondering if I was hearing impaired.

"What the heck is a *leedurts*?" I asked, even more confused.

To my shock, my question seemed to genuinely offend him.

"It's Liderc, not *leedurts*. And you should know. You hatched me," he said, sounding annoyed.

"I did no such thing!" I exclaimed. "Your egg started cracking all over the place, scaring the bejeezus out of me. I mean, fine, I did drop it. But it was already almost open. I just brought my ex-roommate's weird stone-egg-thingy home and put it in a bowl."

"You held me under your armpit for a couple of hours," he countered, crossing his muscular arms over his broad chest in a defiant fashion.

"Well, yeah…" I replied hesitantly while adjusting the towel a bit more securely around me. "I had to carry you out of our old place, and all my bags were full. It was the only spot left for me to carry you. I mean, what else was I supposed to do? Stick your egg into my vagina?"

Far from being offended by my increasingly aggravated pitch the more I spoke, Vazul seemed amused and also quite dubious. He pursed his lips and appeared to give my last comment a serious thought.

"Sheltering my egg inside your vagina is quite an interesting thought. Sadly, that wouldn't have allowed you to summon me. A Liderc must be held under your armpit in order to hatch."

"What the hell kind of crazy shit is this?!" I exclaimed, flabbergasted.

"Don't play coy," Vazul replied, this time appearing to be losing patience with what he clearly seemed to think was me pretending ignorance. "No one holds a black egg under their armpit for hours just for fun. There's nothing wrong with wanting your own sex demon and obedient servant. Why are you playing these games?"

"A sex demon?!" I exclaimed, taking another involuntary step backward. "Whoa! Are you an incubus?!"

He huffed and glared at me as if I had said something offensive. "I'm far superior to an incubus. As I've said multiple times now, I am a Liderc."

"And what the hell is that?" I insisted, also starting to get irritated.

He opened his mouth to answer only to be interrupted by the sound of my phone ringing. Startled, I yelped and pressed my palm to my chest. I wasn't normally this jumpy, but there was nothing normal about my current situation.

And yet, that ring was the biggest blessing. It was Sophia's ringtone. If anyone could help guide me with this current mess, it was her.

"Stay put!" I ordered while pointing a menacing finger at Vazul. "Don't do anything demonic while I answer my call. Just stay right where you are."

He gave me that unimpressed look again as I slowly backed away before running up the stairs to grab my phone. The whole time, I kept glancing over my shoulder, relieved that he obediently stayed right in front of the door, his red eyes never straying from me.

CHAPTER 2
CORAL

I nearly broke my neck dashing into the bathroom to retrieve my phone before I missed the call. I answered and made a beeline for my closet to pull out some clothes.

"Sophia, help!" I exclaimed in lieu of greeting.

"Hey, Coral. What's going on?" she asked with a sliver of worry in her voice.

I quickly told her what had happened as I slipped on some panties and a bustier tank top before taking a swift peek outside over the railing to make sure Vazul had not moved. Thankfully, he was still glued in place, a grumpy expression plastered all over his handsome face.

I hurried back into my bedroom to put on a skirt and a pair of sandals.

"Holy shit! Angie is going to lose it when she finds out you got her Liderc!" Sophia exclaimed with the strangest mix of sympathy and that morbid excitement people got whenever they had just heard a juicy piece of gossip.

"What is he? And why the hell did she leave him behind?" I asked in a whispered voice while stealing the occasional glance outside.

"He's a sex demon. Angie tried to hatch him for weeks... months actually. But the egg never did. She was livid for a long time and eventually lost interest," Sophia explained in a conspiratorial tone.

"Why would she want a sex demon?!" I asked, genuinely baffled. "She has men falling all over themselves to get in her panties... when she even bothers wearing any. So what gives?"

Sophia snorted. Angelique's promiscuity was legendary. Being comfortable with our own sexuality, we weren't ones to slut shame anyone. However, when you shared an apartment with a roommate that constantly had a parade of partners at every hour of the day carrying on loudly, it got grating fast.

"Well obviously, sex with one of them has to be off the charts. But what she really wants is the ultimate servant he represents," Sophia said in a more serious tone. "A Liderc will do absolutely anything you ask. You can pile however many chores on him as you want, and he'll gladly do it. In fact, he needs it."

I stiffened, taken aback by that comment. "What do you mean by he needs it?"

"A Liderc cannot stay idle. If you do not give him enough work, he'll cause mischief. If you're lucky, it will be to your benefit. But more likely than not, it will be to your detriment as a punishment for neglecting him."

My mind raced with all the crazy ways he could potentially 'punish' me for not giving him enough chores.

"How do I get rid of him? There's no circle to send him back, and he vanished the remains of his egg," I said, my voice thick with tension as I went back out to check on the demon.

"Why the fuck would you do that?" Sophia exclaimed, genuinely shocked.

"Isn't it obvious?" I whispered, my stomach knotting as I noticed Vazul's eyes were now glowing a bright, angry red.

I backed away from the railing located only a couple of meters from my room. For all I knew, he had insanely acute hearing and was catching everything we were saying even with me retreating back to my room or whispering.

"He's a sex demon!" I exclaimed in a self-evident tone. "Don't they leech the life out of their lovers?"

"Well yeah," Sophia conceded reluctantly. "But it's not overnight. They only drain a tiny fraction. A good master can keep his demon for decades."

"A tiny bit is already a bit too much! I'm only twenty-seven. I'm not keeling over in ten or twenty years just to have some awesome sex with a demon! And why are his eyes glowing?"

"Glowing how?" she asked.

"Just glowing. Previously, they were just dark red. Now, they are a brighter shade and luminous," I said nervously before sneaking back out.

My heart dropped when I met his gaze. The glow had significantly increased, illuminating his entire face with a terrifying red haze. The corner of his mouth had quirked into the beginning of a snarl.

"Okay, this is not good. It's glowing really heavily," I said nervously.

"He's upset because you're leaving him idle. Give him something to do," Sophia replied.

"Something like what?" I asked, my heart pounding as he clearly was growing angrier by the second.

"Any chore… I don't know. Tell him to sweep the floor!"

"The floor?! I don't want to—"

A low, menacing growl rose from downstairs. Vazul was staring at me with his fangs bared. They looked even longer than before, and vicious claws now jutted from his fingertips. By the way his body was tense and slightly leaning forward, he didn't look like someone about to cause mischief. He looked like a predator about to go for the kill.

"Oh shit!" I whispered before raising my voice and shouting to him in a far less assured voice than I would have wanted.

"While you wait for me to be done, could you sweep the floor?"

I braced, expecting him to release a banshee screech, for his handsome face to suddenly split in half revealing a nightmarish mouth filled with teeth as he lunged at me in rabid rage that I would issue such an outrageous demand.

To my shock, the terrifying glow instantly faded, his body relaxed, and his snarl melted into a smile. I gaped in disbelief as he made a beeline for what I believed was the broom closet, but I couldn't be certain from this angle. Seconds later he returned with the broom and got to work, starting at the front door.

"Are you fucking kidding me?!" I whispered, flabbergasted.

The distant sound of a voice startled me, and I realized that I'd been holding the phone by my hip, too shocked to remember I was having a conversation. I placed the phone back next to my ear.

"Is this shit for real?" I asked Sophia.

She chuckled. "Yep. That's all Lidercs do. They work, acquire wealth for their masters, and fuck them into next week. You hit the jackpot!"

"This is madness!"

"No, girl. It's freaking awesome. But I have to go," Sophia replied. "I was just confirming that you had gotten Angie's stuff out. We don't want to get on Mrs. Hopkins' bad side. But the wedding is starting."

"How do I get rid of him?" I asked, panicked.

"You don't! Just enjoy the best ride of your life," Sophia replied in a singsong voice. "Talk to you later!"

Before I could speak another word, she hung up.

"Fuck my life," I muttered, unsure what to do.

Taking a deep breath, I climbed back down the stairs to check up on my demon. The floors had not actually been particularly dirty as I took great pride in keeping my house clean. But he still managed to gather a notable amount of dust. As soon as he noticed me, the peaceful expression on his face shifted to one of blatant disappointment.

"You got dressed," he said in that disapproving tone I was starting to grow familiar with.

"Of course I did," I replied with a hint of defiance.

"Way to ruin the view," he muttered while continuing to thoroughly perform his chore.

I wanted to chastise him and probably should, too. However, I couldn't deny feeling utterly flattered that he should find me so attractive. Then again, maybe it was just a matter of being annoyed by the extra obstacles to him getting what he wanted.

But he did comment about appreciating the view.

I immediately berated myself that my stupid mind would be dwelling over this nonsense instead of trying to solve my current predicament.

"You can stop cleaning the floor," I said, still mortified that I even gave him that task to begin with.

To my shock, he glared at me as if I had just insulted him.

"Absolutely not! My task is not completed!"

I gaped at him, unsure how to respond to that.

"Oookay," I said at last while he continued to move around, swiftly performing his task with impressive efficiency. "But you also need clothes. Except, I can't walk you around town. People will freak out if they see a demon," I added sheepishly.

He snorted with a slightly disdainful expression. "I'm a Liderc, remember? I can shift my appearance to whatever you want me to be. For example, like this."

My jaw dropped as his skin appeared to melt almost as if he was a wax figure, and his entire body shifted. He gained a bit more body mass, with broader shoulders and thicker muscles. His original height—which I guessed to be around 6'4, grew slightly by a couple of inches. His charcoal skin shifted to the most scrumptious dark brown, a couple of shades darker than mine. He leveled hazel eyes on me sparkling with a victorious glimmer as he smiled at me with the godly face that had featured prominently in many a raunchy dream.

"How did you know?" I whispered, dumbfounded.

He gave me a smug smirk. "Once again, it appears I must remind you that I'm a Liderc. I know every person's deepest fantasies. How else am I supposed to please them?"

"Okay, TMI!" I said, raising my hands in an arresting gesture while shaking my head.

"TMI?" he echoed, tilting his head to the side with an inquisitive expression.

"Too much information," I replied.

However, my stupid mind immediately started wondering what kind of freaky things he might see about me. Beyond the kinks I already knew about myself, what else might my subconscious secretly harbor and that could be laid bare to this demon, unbeknownst to me?

Vazul's grin broadening as he wiggled his eyebrows in a conspiratorial fashion only increased my mortification. And then, his massive black dick grew hard.

"STOP THAT!" I exclaimed, averting my eyes.

"Stop thinking dirty stuff, and my body won't have the natural reaction they prompt," Vazul said nonchalantly with a shrug.

"Then stop reading my mind! I cannot help what crazy thoughts it concocts!" I replied defensively.

"I'm not reading it. You're loudly projecting your wishes because your subconscious wants me to do something about it," he replied tauntingly.

Obviously, I was too clueless about his kind to know whether his response was truthful or just a manipulation. Either way, this entire situation sucked hairy donkey balls.

"Fuck my life," I muttered.

"Your life?" he responded with an amused expression. "I cannot do that. But you, on the other hand—"

"Enough!" I exclaimed, throwing my hands in the air. "What the fuck am I supposed to do with you?"

"Many things, Mistress. Want me to show you?" he asked in an obnoxiously suggestive fashion.

"GAH!" I growled in aggravation before stomping off to my workshop.

His smug chuckle followed me until I slammed the door behind me. I stood looking at all the work that awaited me and had been derailed by this day's entire mess. I groaned inwardly, feeling overwhelmed. I was so close to finishing, yet still so far away.

Launching my miniature and furniture store had been a life-long dream of mine. I was only a couple of weeks away from the grand opening. I deliberately scheduled it to fall only a couple of days after the massive miniatures fair which would take place next week. I hoped to get a ton of exposure as an exhibitor over there. Hopefully, I'd make enough sales to bring in a substantial cash influx that would help tide me over during the first few months as I established my business.

As always, I had been too ambitious. My crazy imagination was my eternal downfall. The entire collection revolved around the fair's "Haunted Victorian Era" theme. I had created multiple miniature mansions, businesses, streets, parks, and even a fairground. Each building or outdoor space was divided into rooms or areas that conveyed part of the story of the haunting.

The wide table at the back overflowed with individual props people could buy to populate or decorate their own miniature worlds, ranging from tiny Victorian furniture to characters with era-appropriate garbs and hairdos, pets, carriages, plants, and everything else in-between. Many of these items were initially meant to be a part of my other creations but ended up not truly fitting.

But my main creations—and what I intended to build my business around—were standard size furniture with embedded miniatures. After all, bookshelves weren't the only ones who deserved elevating with book nook inserts. My showstopper was my coffee table with an alchemist's laboratory built inside. The thick glass top allowed us to enjoy the highly detailed beauty of the room, with interactive elements like electric lights and tesla coils. I had designed the table in a way that you could change the built-in miniature to a different theme, like a library, a mysterious alley, etc. For the fair, the second built-in option was a haunted Victorian street.

Today's events completely trashed my plans. Fetching Angie's stuff wasted my entire morning. Now, I was dealing with a freaking demon instead of ordering the missing material and getting back to work to complete my collection in time. With my ADHD, I couldn't even decide what I should prioritize first.

I hated the thought of Vazul leering at Angie in any way. That he might look at her naked body the way he had done with mine just whipped my blood into a primal rage. What the fuck was wrong with me? Was he using some sort of power to make me want him?

I peered at my laptop sitting on my desk. Without giving it a second thought, I headed straight for it, plopped my butt on my chair, and tried to do some research on his demonic breed. To my dismay, nothing popped up that matched the name both Vazul and Sophia had stated for his species. I tried different spellings for *leedurts*, *leedirts*, *leederts*, and even iterations with a single 'e' in the first syllable, to no avail. And if I searched for sex demons, every single result would speak of an incubus, a succubus, or the human-demon hybrid offspring called a cambion.

Maybe I should try to call Angie again.

The instant ick and nearly possessive anger that thought triggered within me took me aback. There was no question Angie would be all over him the minute she found out the egg hatched. She just liked hoarding things and slapping a stamp of ownership on anything even remotely unique, so that she could flaunt how she had things no one else did. But it was an even more irrational emotion that prompted such a strong response from me.

Before I could spiral into that bottomless pit of indecisiveness that would keep me paralyzed, the door opened, startling me. Totally unfazed, as if he'd just barged into his own office, Vazul started sweeping the floor. He had gone back to his default demonic appearance.

I glared at him, my conflicting emotions too rattled for me to sort them out.

"Okay, you really need clothes," I grumbled.

He paused his sweeping to look at me, then spread his arms wide before glancing down at himself.

"And ruin this awesome view?" he asked.

I scrunched my face. "Egotistical much?"

He shrugged. "Not ego, more like confidence rooted in facts."

I rolled my eyes, looking for a sharp comeback to take him down a peg or two. However, seeing him glance at my miniatures collection then wrinkling his nose in an unimpressed fashion instantly had my back stiffen.

"Ugh! Such a dreadful execution of a brilliant idea," he mused aloud.

"Wow! Why don't you just come out and say how you really feel?" I exclaimed, deeply wounded.

"I just did," he replied in a factual manner, giving me a baffled look as if he was questioning my intelligence.

I poured my heart and soul into this project. Claiming that I had shed blood, sweat, and tears over this would not be a cliche or understatement. To have it so brutally trashed was devastating.

"Well that was unbelievably rude and hurtful," I said in a clipped tone, floored that he should be so oblivious.

He tilted his head to the side, confused. "You want me to lie?"

I gaped at him. Was he truly this obtuse or just a douchebag?

"Get out," I snapped.

"I haven't cleaned—"

"GET OUT!" I shouted, pointing angrily at the door.

He made a face as if I was the most illogical creature he'd ever encountered, huffed, then exited the room. I slumped against the backrest of my chair and heaved a sigh, defeated.

CHAPTER 3
VAZUL

I swept the upstairs floors with far more strength than necessary, a clear sign of my aggravation. Then again, uneasiness might be a more appropriate word, which greatly bothered me. I definitely wasn't digging the emotions emanating from my Coral. Even dampened by the distance, they tasted foul compared to those she expressed earlier.

I loved the repressed desire and blossoming fascination she felt towards me. There was nothing more delectable to me than to break the last resistance of a target eager to be conquered. And my Mistress wanted me to do all kinds of unspeakable things to her, once her consciousness reconciled with the secret wishes of her subconscious.

Why was she so damn butt hurt? I spoke honestly. The entire concept of her project was indeed brilliant. A simple glimpse sufficed for me to appreciate the creativity, the impeccable story-telling, the innovative approach she took with some of the furniture, and the harmonious flow of each element she created. It was truly wonderful. But the execution was beyond dreadful. The finishing was lacking. Some of the miniature furniture wasn't properly scaled, or not perfectly even. The materials she used for the shingles on the roof or to make the fake blankets were abysmal.

Instead of kicking me out, Coral should have thanked me for pointing out that her concept could be improved, then asked me to fix it. After all, that was the whole point of having a Liderc.

But she's clueless about my kind.

How is that even possible? She hatched me. You didn't waltz around with an egg under your armpit for hours just for fun. Granted, she claimed she had just retrieved it with nowhere else to put it, but I felt her care for the safety of my egg beckoning me. She feared I had gotten harmed at some point. So how could she claim she had no idea of what I was?

People usually were beside themselves with joy when they successfully hatched one of us. They understood our worth and how invaluable an asset we could be. But she didn't want me. She genuinely wanted to get rid of me and cast me back from whence I came.

That truly hurt my feelings—something I never thought one such as I would ever say.

Obviously, she lusted for me. How could she not? Beyond the fact that I knew myself to naturally be very attractive, I was a sex demon. Our basic aura instinctively drew people to us. Despite that, she was still considering getting rid of me. And my words only fanned that flame.

That won't do.

After all, I chose her, too. There was a reason so many aspirants failed to secure their own Lidercs. I wouldn't be so easily dismissed. Anyway, she would soon find out it wasn't as simple a task to accomplish. And I would make it even more impossible for her to achieve such a ridiculous goal. I was *her* Liderc, and she was *my* Mistress. No one would take away what was rightfully mine without my consent. And I did not consent to parting with her.

Maybe I should just apologize...

But she ordered me to get out. However much I disagreed with any of her commands, I had to obey. Otherwise, I would have pointed out how unreasonable she was being. Therefore, I had to comply.

She didn't forbid me from returning.

When it came to exploiting loopholes, demons and other netherworld beings excelled at finding the cracks they could slip through. An almost malicious grin stretched my lips before another wave of my Mistress' conflicting emotions irked me again.

She kept going from distress to determination, defeat to hope, annoyance to confusion, and then right back to the beginning. I wanted to run back downstairs, spank the silly out of her, fuck her senseless to remind her of what a treasure she now possessed in me, then fix the messy parts of her project while she basked in the afterglow.

Pleased with that plan, I hurried through my chore so that I could go back to my Coral. Just as I was about to head downstairs, I caught my reflection in her mirror.

Fuck, I do look mighty fine!

I struck a couple of poses, admiring the ridges of my cock and how my inner fire glowed between some of the creases on demand. Thinking how insane with pleasure it would make my woman had me stiffening in seconds.

But she's annoyed with my nudity.

I instantly balked at the thought of covering up. How was I to properly entice her without flaunting all that I had to offer?

You're more than just a hot body.

True. I was far more. In fact, I was everything she didn't even know she wanted or needed. It struck me then that I was approaching this all wrong. She didn't understand what I was. Therefore, my bluntness distressed her. Her emotions clearly indicated that she needed to be cheered up before we could engage in a more rational conversation that would eventually help lower her infuriating barriers. Stepping all over her bound-aries by strutting back into her workshop with my overly eager cock on full display wouldn't earn me any favors.

I rummaged through her wardrobe and drawers, careful to put everything back exactly in its place—although I did realign a few things that weren't perfectly positioned. Her slender frame didn't agree with my much more muscular stature when it came to clothing apparel. I loved everything in her closet, which I already pictured how perfectly they would hug the scrumptious curves of her body. And that butt of hers…!

My mouth watered just reminiscing about how perfectly round and perky it had felt beneath my palm when I checked how much she had bruised it with that absurd fall. I still wanted to roll my eyes at the thought of her trying to run away from me.

After a bit more rummaging, I finally found the perfect outfit. Beyond the fact that it was the only thing that fit, it looked so ridiculous on me that it would undoubtedly provide the result I was aiming for.

I made my way back downstairs, barefoot and shirtless. The strangest thrill coursed down my spine as I knocked on the door and then swiftly opened to prevent her from sending me away before she saw me.

Right on cue, she jerked her head towards the door with an angry expression.

"I said go a… What the fuck?!" she exclaimed upon taking in my appearance.

It took every ounce of my willpower not to burst out laugh-ing. Still, I couldn't help a smug smile when her anger gave way to shock before she started giggling. The unpleasant taint of her previous emotions faded, bringing back the delightful taste I was already becoming addicted to.

"What the hell are you wearing?" Coral asked with disbelief, still chuckling.

"You said I needed to put some clothes on. So I did. Not

exactly my aesthetic, but it fits reasonably well, does it not?" I asked, batting my eyelashes before striking a pose, pivoting to give her a 360 view, and then striking a final pose.

She chuckled again. Fuck, I wanted to feast on those emotions! But as feeding made my eyes glow, I didn't want to break this fragile truce by being too greedy.

"Right, but this? A pink tutu on a muscular sex demon is beyond silly," she replied in a gently chastising tone.

"But it made you laugh," I said matter-of-factly. "Your happy emotions are pleasant and much nicer than what you were broadcasting earlier."

Her smile instantly vanished, and she glared at me, her resentment rearing its ugly head again.

"Then you shouldn't have taken a massive shit on my work," she snapped, folding her arms angrily over her chest.

"I didn't shit on your work," I said firmly. "Didn't I state that the concept was brilliant? Because it absolutely is, so is the creativity. But the execution is lacking. I apologize if my wording offended you. I am used to being blunt, not necessarily diplomatic. Here, let me show you."

Coral scrunched her face, seeming unsure as to whether she was willing to forgive me just yet. However, she seemed somewhat mollified by the sincerity in my voice. She rose from her work desk where she had apparently been ordering materials. I gestured for her to approach as I hovered over the central table where many of the mostly completed miniature buildings were sitting.

"The wallpaper in that living area is stunning. But you can see over there that it isn't straight. It has to be redone as the wall decorations that you placed, especially those paintings, really highlight the flaws," I explained in as kind a tone as I could muster. "The scale of this couch is deceptively perfect in the context of this room. But when you look at the adjacent one on the other side of the partition wall, you can see the significant discrepancy. The living room seems to house a giant while the study seems to be home to a dwarf. Consistency is a must."

Coral's shoulders slouched. "I know. That couch is part of my long list of things to fix and redo."

I gave her an approving smile. "Good. There are few tricks I will gladly share with you that can help expedite the process."

I then pointed to the dining room of the haunted mansion.

"This table is a beautiful design, perfect scale, and fully appropriate for the setting and era. However, all I see is that... chair at the head of the table."

I barely caught myself before I would have said *horrendous* chair instead. That would have completely defeated my reconciliation efforts.

I picked up the chair, grabbed a metal nail file, then began to sand down the excess of material that kept the legs uneven, with one of them slightly thicker than the other three. Once done, I put it back inside the open-faced miniature house then glanced at her.

"Isn't it better now?" I asked in a gentle voice.

She made a face then nodded. "Those stupid legs always give me a hard time."

"The finishing is lacking but makes a huge difference," I said. "Although better, I would still want to varnish all of the chairs and table in a warmer brown color to elevate them further."

I then waved at the upper floor of the three-story dollhouse, drawing her attention to what appeared to be the master bedroom. She'd created a pretty throw with a soft felt fabric that made it look stiff.

"This throw? Great idea, wonderful color and placement that brings life and warmth to the room. But it's too stiff to feel natural. Here's what I would have done instead," I explained pointing at it.

I loved that, despite feeling a little bummed out with me

highlighting the flaws, my Mistress still listened with an open-minded curiosity. I hurried over to the counter to the left of the door where many of her crafting materials were organized in a rather pleasant fashion. As I had obsessive-compulsive tendencies when it came to order and perfection, this pleased me.

Then again, I had to silence my itch to move one of her bead containers a couple of millimeters to the right so that it would be evenly spaced with the others...

I picked up a pin from a cushion, and a forest green ball of lace thin yarn. My female's heightened curiosity catered to my exhibitionist tendencies, in this instance not in a sexual manner, but just my shameless need to show off my many skills and talents.

I put the yarn on the display table next to the dollhouse, then held the pin between two fingers, the pointy tip up. Using my right index finger, I summoned my fire. Coral gasped as my fingertip turned an angry shade of red, before a flame danced around it. Pressing my finger on the back of the sharp point of the pin, I bent it so that it would form a hook. I then reclaimed the lingering heat from the pin, instantly cooling it before dowsing my fire. My task completed, I waved my newly improvised miniature crochet needle in a victorious fashion before my Mistress.

The stunned look of wonder on her face stroked my ego to no end. I reveled in the fascinated and excited emotions swirling around her as I pulled the thin thread of the yarn and started crocheting the most delicate throw with some lace patterns in the middle.

"Are you fucking kidding me!" Coral whispered to herself in complete disbelief as the fabric came to life before her very eyes.

It only took me minutes to complete my task before I carefully placed it on top of the bed. I turned back to look at her with a smug expression. Her gaze lingered in awe on the throw before she peered at me.

"This is beautiful," she said in a subdued voice filled with admiration and a hint of sadness that didn't sit well with me. "I'd love to do things like this, but I don't have the time, the skill, or the focus. I know what I want to do, and how I want to do it. But my stupid mind just wanders off, gets distracted, and then I end up scrambling trying to get things done."

"Your mind isn't stupid, it is brilliantly imaginative. What you have created isn't just a set of miniatures, it is an emotion, a journey, a tale people will want to immerse themselves in. You just need a little nudge to get it to a level worthy of your vision. And that's where I come in."

"I can't make you fix my crap!" she exclaimed, scandalized.

If not for the embarrassment I perceived for her actually wishing and hoping I would grant her my help, I might have been offended. But the silly female genuinely felt horrible at the thought of exploiting me. My Coral was adorably clueless.

"Yes you can, and I demand no less," I said in a stern voice. "I am your Liderc. Fixing things and making your life better is my sole purpose. Denying me would not only be an insult but downright cruel."

She blinked, unsure how to respond.

"I don't want to turn you into a slave," she said carefully.

I gave her the 'seriously?' look. "I'm a Liderc. We 'need' to be kept busy to thrive. I thought you would have looked it up by now."

"I tried!" she exclaimed, throwing her hands up. "There is no such thing as a *leederts* or *leedairts*, however you pronounce it. Look!"

Coral walked back to her laptop and switched to a different tab of her browser where her search was still on full display. I rolled my eyes at the spelling, even as a part of me found it unbelievably cute.

"Right. You wouldn't find it with that spelling. It is a

Hungarian word. So while it is pronounced *leedairts*, it's actually spelled L-i-d-e-r-c," I said teasingly.

Her jaw dropped as she stared at me for a few seconds before proceeding to type the word with the appropriate spelling. A whole bunch of results now populated the screen. She muttered a series of swear words that had me chuckling.

"Now read up," I ordered, showing myself rather ballsy considering I should be the servant.

A part of me wondered why I was being so candid with her. Coral's cluelessness provided me with a golden opportunity to abuse the situation. And yet, for a reason I couldn't explain, I wanted her to fully understand who and what I was, and wholly accept me. Over the centuries, I had served other masters, but none had ever felt like her. They'd been greedy and self-serving, seeing me as property to be used with complete disregard for my own wishes. At a visceral level, I understood that this woman was different. In truth, it was that difference that had beckoned me and convinced me to hatch.

Coral gave me a hesitant look before complying. The whole time, I drank in each of her emotions, studying her reactions to what it revealed about my kind, including our strengths and weaknesses.

"Wait. You're going to sit on my chest, suffocating me and sucking my lifeforce while I sleep?!" she exclaimed, horrified.

I chuckled. "Only if you don't keep me busy enough or feed me," I deadpanned.

She mumbled something unintelligible then resumed reading.

"What's the thing about the chicken foot?" she asked moments later while peering at my legs.

I snorted. "Lesser Lidercs will have a chicken foot that they cannot hide, even when they shift. I am not one of them. You have the elite among our peers at your service."

It was her turn to snort at the pompous way in which I spoke those words.

"Your ego knows no bounds."

"Is it ego when it is merely a statement of fact?" I mused aloud with an exaggerated introspective expression.

She laughed again and shook her head as if I was a hopeless case. Coral finished reading from a couple of different sites before pivoting on her desk chair to study my features.

"So you're mine since I hatched you. I must give you chores or tasks to do, otherwise you will go crazy. You must obey any order I give you, regardless of how you feel about it. Your main goal is to make my life easier and help enrich me. You can give me the wildest sex I ever could have hoped for. And the only way for us to part ways is either for me to die, or me giving you such an impossible task to accomplish that you will kill yourself trying. Did I get all of that right?"

"You did," I said with a nod.

"That's every shade of fucked up!" Coral exclaimed.

"No, Mistress. That's every shade of awesome. You're about to have everything you ever wanted with the aid of yours truly, while having mind-blowing sex on demand. What more could you ask for?"

"Well… When you put it that way," she conceded sheepishly.

I rested my palms on the armrests of her chair, leaning forward in a seductive fashion.

"So what were you saying about getting rid of me?" I taunted.

"I don't remember," she replied, her eyes locked on my lips as the delicious scent of her arousal timidly awakened.

I purred and leaned even closer, my lips a hair's breadth from hers. Just as I was about to go for the kiss, Coral placed her palms on my chest and pushed me back.

"But I'm not keeping you dressed like that!" she retorted, in what I knew to be one last ditch effort to resist temptation.

I glanced at the ridiculous tutu still hiding my modesty and summarily yanked it down, letting it fall to my feet.

"Then keep me as I am, undressed and all yours."

CHAPTER 4
CORAL

Lord have mercy! Vazul was the biggest temptation I had ever faced. Every fiber of my being was shouting at me to just freaking enjoy this unexpected gift from above. Well, technically, it was rather a gift from below. My mind raced with all the reasons why this was a bad idea. Simultaneously, the wicked little voice that always berated me for being such a lame ass party pooper was yelling at me to seize the day... and this fine demon's cock.

I was comfortable with my sexuality. While I didn't sleep around, I had no qualms about partaking in some consensual skin on skin time. Vazul was my very own sex demon. Intimacy with him would be off the charts. So why was I holding back? Considering I gave zero shits what other people thought about me, why not indulge in what I craved?

I couldn't tell if the look on my face, my body language, or his ability to read emotions gave away the moment I finally caved in. One minute, he was staring at me in his glorious nudity, and the next, his hands were on my thighs, caressing a path up my short red skirt as he leaned forward to claim my lips.

His hands were incredibly warm, just like his mouth, but not in an uncomfortable way. The heat seeped into me, making me instantly relaxed, even as it heated my blood. A dull throbbing awakened between my thighs as his tongue teased the seam of my mouth, requesting entry. I didn't resist, welcoming his invading tongue. His warm breath sent a tingling down my throat. I couldn't describe the sensation as I was too busy with his delightful taste of peach and cinnamon as our tongues mingled.

His searing hands settled on my behind, and he lifted me up. I gasped against his lips and instinctively wrapped my arms and legs around him. A thrill coursed through me when I felt a stiff rod pressing against my stomach as he carried me across the room. To my shock, he didn't settle me down on the comfy cushions of the couch in the workshop but sat me on the right arm instead facing outward.

Vazul's hands were all over me, groping, caressing, exploring with the possessiveness of a conqueror. I never even realized when he released the four hooks of my tank top, which attached at the back like a bra. The fabric rubbed against my stomach as he pulled it off and tossed it somewhere behind him. With one hand holding my nape, Vazul broke the kiss, his fangs gently grazing the line of my jaw, then following a path down the curve of my neck. He licked my clavicles, tracing swirling patterns with the tip of his tongue before pursuing his journey down to the aching buds of my nipples.

But just as he was about to wrap his mouth around the left one, I stiffened and pushed back on his shoulders as a thought crossed my mind.

"Wait! You're not going to leech me while we play naughty, right?" I asked.

My stomach dropped when he didn't immediately say no.

"I need to feed. Hatching requires a lot of energy," he said in a neutral voice.

"Right, but not by draining my lifeforce, correct?" I insisted.

My heart broke when he just stared at me. I pushed back further on his shoulders, trying to ignore the dull throbbing between my thighs, the hollowness screaming to be filled, and the wretched voice at the back of my head shouting that just a little leeching this once wasn't such a big deal. After all, Sophia said as much.

"I'm sorry," I said, proud of myself for not recklessly giving in. "This is a deal breaker for me. I mean, you're crazy hot. And I definitely want to get down and dirty with you. But not at the cost of dying early."

"It won't kill you overnight," he argued, as if that was self-evident.

"Maybe not overnight, but it will still shorten my lifespan. Correct?" I asked, daring him to deny it.

He pursed his lips, looking somewhat disgruntled before giving me a stiff nod.

"Yes, it will."

"Theeeeen that's a hard pass for me," I said, trying to gently push him aside while sliding down the edge of the armrest of the couch.

Vazul took a step closer, blocking me in, his right hand tightening on my nape while the other gripped my right butt cheek.

"Fine, I won't drain you," he growled, visibly displeased.

"How do I know you're not lying to get what you want?" I challenged, my eyes flicking between his.

He gave me an offended look. "You are my Mistress. I cannot lie to you. If I say I won't drain you, then I am sworn to uphold my word."

I couldn't tell if I was being naive or just allowing myself to be swayed because he was saying what I wanted to hear, but I believed him. Instantly, a different type of unease swelled within me.

"But will you starve if you don't?" I asked timidly.

He shook his head, still looking a bit disgruntled. For some stupid reason, he reminded me of a man expecting a fancy meal and being served a stir fry and steamed rice instead of the big fat steak with potatoes he'd been salivating for.

"No. I can survive on emotions. They're not as filling and won't make me as powerful, but it will sustain me."

"And that doesn't drain my lifeforce and won't make me die earlier?" I asked, wanting to make sure there was no misunderstanding.

"No, it will not. It is entirely harmless for you. It just means I will have to make you come harder and more often to be sated," he said with a shrug.

I blinked. "And that's a problem, how? Aren't you a sex demon?"

He snorted, his aggravation fading away while the most lascivious expression descended over his handsome features.

"I am. And right now, I am famished. Prepared to scream for me, Mistress."

His hand on my nape glided up to fist my hair. He yanked my head back with just enough force to give it the right type of sting even as his mouth latched onto my nipple. The searing heat of his lips sucking on my hardening little nubs reawakened the throbbing that had begun to dull during our conversation.

I gasped when his hand on my butt slipped to my front with a boldness that left me reeling. He didn't pussyfoot around, tease, or hover. Vazul went straight for gold, shoving the slim fabric of my panties to the side before fingering my slit. A violent shiver coursed through me when an unnatural heat began spreading along my inner walls as his fingers dipped inside of me. I held onto his shoulders, my head thrown back as sighs of delight tumbled out of me.

He nipped at my nipple, then immediately soothed the slight pain with a lick before sucking on it again. How the fuck did he manage to make it feel as if it was my clit he was tending to? Except, it was his thumb flicking it while two fingers dipped in and out of me. It took me a moment to realize what was causing the strange sensation over my skin, wherever his body touched me. I glanced down at him, only to see fiery lightning streaks flicking in and out of existence under his skin. The heat they generated acted almost like the gentle caress of ebbing warm water.

A strangled moan escaped me when he repeatedly grazed my sweet spot by crooking his fingers inside me. Intense pleasure began building deep within. As he abandoned my left nipple to pay homage to the right one, I noticed his eyes glowing. It wasn't the angry red shade that had so frightened me earlier. This one had a reassuring silver-blue hue.

I realized he was feeding. As a 'newborn' demon, he undoubtedly had to be starving. The tiny voice of reason at the back of my head whispered I should be freaking out, but a thrill coursed through me instead at that sense of danger.

To my dismay, just as I was beginning to crest, Vazul suddenly yanked his fingers out of me and pulled down both my skirt and panties at the same time. The room spun, and I yelped as he jerked my garments upward, lifting my legs up in the process. I fell backward onto the cushion of the couch, my butt still propped up by the armrest. Before I could regain my bearings, the inferno of Vazul's mouth settled on my clit.

My back arched, and I cried out as he immediately proceeded to devour me like a famished beast. Kneeling next to the couch, his face buried between my thighs, Vazul settled my legs over his shoulders while he feasted. My demon extruded his claws, and raked them over my belly, the length of my thighs, and down my legs in a blazing trail that had me shivering all over.

His tongue fucking me was driving me insane with bliss. I had kissed him. My tongue had swirled around his. But what was thrusting in and out of me right now felt impossibly thick and long. Each time he pulled it out, Vazul slightly tilted his head back, giving my clit a mind-blowing rub that sent electric sparks throughout my nether region.

My climax crashed over me, tearing a sharp cry out of my throat. With a will of their own, my feet kicked up, as violent spasms coursed through me. As pleasure swept me away, I felt Vazul yank his horns free from my grasp. His tongue pulled out of me, and the room spun again. Next thing I knew, I was lying face down on the cushion, ass up.

A slapping sound followed a wondrous sting on my right butt cheek. Still dazed and flying high from my orgasm, I welcomed the spanking Vazul rained on my behind. Each blow resonated directly in my clit. My toes curled, and my skin tingled. I'd always fantasized about a proper spanking. But the couple of partners I had attempted it with in the past had either been too rough, ruining the experience, or too skittish making it a complete let down. But my demon was putting the perfect level of strength for me to feel it without hurting me.

More moisture pulled between my thighs. Had I been the squirter type, there was no doubt he'd be drenched by now. I'd finally gotten back down from my climax when he leaned forward and gave my butt a good nip that had my legs jerking in response. He soothed it with a lick and rubbed his face all over my cheeks with an almost feral growl.

"You have the most beautiful ass, my Coral," he purred in a deep and grumbling voice, almost menacing. "I want to devour you."

My stomach did a backflip in response, then a second one when I felt myself flying upward. It was only once I found myself upside down, staring at the thickest demonic cock that I realized what happened. With my thighs hanging over his shoulders, Vazul buried his face between my legs again and resumed eating me out. He held me with one arm around my back. With his freehand, he alternated between spanking my behind and clawing my skin the length of my back. The exquisite burning sensation had goosebumps erupting all over me even as wave after wave of shivers shook my body.

The sweet aroma of the treat before my eyes beckoned me. Despite the overwhelming sensations my demon's ministration stirred within me, I couldn't resist reaching for his stiff cock. It was magnificent, with two coiled ridges, vaguely reminiscent of a thick rope lining the sides of his shaft in a sinewy pattern. A series of bumps, and fanning vertical ridges, adorned the upper side of his length. My inner walls contracted in anticipation at the thought of how those ridges would feel inside me.

I wrapped my hand around it. Fuck, it was massive! And yet, even as I feared how I would be able to take him, a bolt of lust nevertheless exploded in my nether region. I began to stroke him, reveling in the odd sensation of the ridges against my palm. I stared in fascination as a fiery glow pulsated between the creases of his cock, heating my hand in the process.

I leaned forward and tentatively licked the head, which greatly resembled the shape of a human dick. My eyes nearly popped out of my head when the taste of a warm peach cobbler exploded on my taste buds. With a greedy moan, I drew him into my mouth, taking as much of him as I could. The way his body jerked in response hinted that he approved. He didn't need to say more. I immediately bobbed in front of him, my tongue swirling around his unusual length, savoring both his wondrous taste and the sensation of him in my mouth.

Never in a million years would I have believed anyone telling me that I would participate in a sixty-nine with my partner standing up while holding me upside down. That he did it so effortlessly screamed volumes of his strength. But it also revealed how much I implicitly trusted him not to drop me in the throes of passion. Having always been the reasonable and rational one, none of my current behavior made sense. And yet, as I once more neared the edge of bliss, I never felt safer with a lover than with my Liderc.

The movement of my mouth on him became erratic as pleasure quickly overwhelmed me. Vazul suddenly nipping my clit did me in. I screamed with his cock still halfway inside my mouth as I came undone. In the distance, I vaguely heard my demon emit a savage growl, his hold tightening almost painfully around me as if he was fighting not to give in to his own pleasure.

Displaying that same insane strength and control, Vazul lifted me back up as I still shook, swept away by ecstasy. With my back pressed to his chest, he folded my legs against my own chest, keeping me twisted like a pretzel, unable to do anything but submit to whatever he pleased. Seeing how I was still riding the waves of bliss, he wouldn't have met any resistance on my part.

Just like he had done when he held me upside down in that crazy sixty-nine, Vazul held me against his chest with a single arm. With his free hand, he rubbed my clit, prolonging my orgasm for a while longer until I slowly came back to reality. And then, I felt his thick head probe my opening. A sliver of fear coursed through me that I might not be able to take him. Sure enough, my inner walls resisted his invasion. The burning feeling of his fingers massaging my little nub distracted me from the discomfort as he gradually inserted himself with shallow thrusts.

And then my body yielded.

A strangled moan vibrated in my throat as he filled me to the brim. He remained still for a few moments to let me adjust to his girth. His fingers on my clit, his lips on my nape, and the fiery streaks under his skin giving me heated wave-like caresses engulfed me in the most delightful maelstrom of sensations.

Soon, my inner walls began contracting around his cock with a will of their own, giving my demon lover the go ahead. That message was apparently conveyed loud and clear as Vazul immediately started thrusting into me. My eyes instantly rolled to the back of my head. My brain couldn't process the overwhelming sensation of his ridges caressing my inner walls and striking my G-spot with deadly precision with each motion—whether going in or out.

In no time, Vazul was pounding into me, wrecking me with pleasure too intense to bear. His fingers on my clit all but shoved me over the finish line in record speed. My climax slammed into me with such violence, not a single sound came out of me. My mouth opened in a silent O, and my body seized before going limp.

"You are mine, Mistress. All of you is mine!" Vazul hissed in a menacing fashion.

I couldn't respond as my consciousness hovered in an indistinct place between reality and oblivion as my demon's thick cock continued to destroy me. A glowing light at the edge of my vision indicated that he was feeding from the tsunami of ecstasy pouring out of me even as he kissed and nipped the feverish skin of my neck and shoulder.

In French, they called an orgasm 'la petite mort' which meant the little death due to that floating sensation and almost loss of consciousness that accompanied that ultimate bliss. And right now, I truly felt at the edge of the most exquisite death as my demonic lover ravaged me.

Vazul suddenly roared. He slammed his cock deep, and the searing heat of his seed shot inside of me, burning me to cinders. A bright light exploded before my eyes as a sharp pain pierced my neck, followed by liquid bliss. My brain realized my Liderc sank his fangs into me, but my ultimate climax claimed me. I cried out and surrendered to ecstasy even as a veil of darkness cast me down into oblivion.

~

An hour after the most unusual romp of my life, my girly bits were still singing. Vazul preening like a peacock made me want to smack the back of his head. And yet, he had every right to feel this cocky and smug. My sex demon knew how to fuck.

But is he always this acrobatic?

I'd always wished to try weirder positions but never felt safe enough with anyone. My Liderc just went balls to the wall with it. And I couldn't complain. Although I also wanted the more traditional stuff, and especially cuddling after the fact, I couldn't wait to see what else he had in store for me.

However, the garage had finally called to inform me that my car was ready. Their chauffeur service was on their way to pick me up to go get it back. It felt odd to leave Vazul here all by himself, not that I worried he would do anything funky.

"Stop fretting so much, Mistress. I'll work on your miniatures while you're gone," he said, drawing me into his embrace.

Unlike me, Vazul remained naked after our little tussle. Feeling his shaft hardening again certainly didn't help. His smirk indicated he knew how much his body against mine affected me.

Asshole.

"You don't have to call me Mistress. You're not my slave. Coral is fine," I grumbled.

He stared at me with a strange glimmer in his eyes mixed with a sliver of what felt like rebellion. I glared at him when he smiled but didn't answer. I suspected it might take me a while to get him to come around on that front.

"I'll be gone awhile," I warned him, trying to remain focused. "I have to make a detour by the shopping mall to grab you some clothes."

He nodded. "Very well. There's plenty for me to do here to keep me busy in your absence."

"Don't strain yourself," I said, unable to fight the guilt that systematically reared its head every time I thought of him doing all that work for me.

His unimpressed look had me scrunching my face again. I didn't know if I would ever fully be at peace with the idea that someone actually craved doing chores or any other form of manual labor.

"Fine. Just so you know, I won't buy too many things today. I'll just get the basic necessities for you. Tomorrow, we can go back together so that you can choose things more to your liking to complete your wardrobe."

"Very well," he said with a smile.

The doorbell startled me.

"He's here! I better get going."

I pulled away from his embrace, grabbed my purse, and hurried out of the workshop. As I entered the main hallway towards the entrance, a familiar ball of fire zipped past me in the strangest déjà vu. Vazul stopped in front of the door and shifted back into his demon form. Fist on his hips, his cock still erect, he glared at me disapprovingly.

"Where's my goodbye kiss?" he demanded.

I snorted. "Haven't you had enough of those already?"

"From you? Never," he said in a self-evident manner.

Cue exploding ovaries. Yeah, I was a sucker for feeling needed and wanted. I didn't know if being a sex demon made it an automatic go to behavior for him, or if he felt compelled to act lovey dovey towards me. But right this instant, I didn't care. His reactions to me seemed genuine, and I loved how he made me feel.

"Fine, you bully," I said playfully while closing the distance between us.

He drew me against him and claimed my mouth with a possessiveness that had my toes curling and my girly bits standing to attention. Fuck, how could he get me this horny so

47

quickly? My pussy was still raw from the most savage ride it had ever experienced before. And yet, here I was aching for more as his wicked tongue plundered my mouth.

His hand slipped over my behind, giving my right cheek a tight squeeze even as he pressed me against his pelvis. My demon loved my butt. I couldn't blame him. Of all my physical attributes, I couldn't deny that my booty was fine as hell.

The bell ringing again had me yelping against his lips. I pushed away from him while he chuckled smugly. I glared at him and flicked his dick as punishment. He gasped, and gave me the weirdest expression halfway between shock, outrage, and amusement.

"See you later. And be a good boy while I'm gone," I said in a singsong voice before hurrying out of the house with his sexy laughter following me.

I picked up my car and drove directly to the mall. The whole drive, I started questioning everything all over again. What the hell was I doing? How did I go from picking up my ex-room-mate's leftover junk to getting my pussy plowed to oblivion by a demon, all in one day?

I don't know jack shit about him.

Granted, everything I read online after he pointed out the proper spelling to me matched what Sophia had said. Frankly, her stating that I would be crazy not to keep him played a major role in lowering my defenses. But this still was nothing like me.

The sex was beyond stellar. I couldn't picture myself ever settling for anyone else after that. There would be no possible comparison. But was he leeching me? He swore he wouldn't, and I didn't feel anything that indicated that he might have been. However, was it something you actually could feel?

What did that mean for the future? Should I eventually meet a man I wanted to settle down with, he would never accept me having a demon lover—not that I would ever want to cheat on my partner. And I strongly suspected that Vazul wouldn't be willing to share me either. It didn't really make sense why it would upset him. After all, as a sex demon, he would likely be down with fucking everything and anything that moved. And yet, at a visceral level, I genuinely believed he would incinerate any male that came sniffing my way.

It's the way he said that I was his.

That thought gave me pause. Right before he came inside of me, he did claim me with a possessiveness that left no room for interpretation. As much as he said that he belonged to me as my loyal servant, my gut told me that he also claimed ownership over me.

What kind of freak am I that this pleases me?

Yeah, with my demon around, there would be no other boyfriend. Anyway, based on what I read—and which he confirmed—the only way for us to separate was if either one of us dies. So I was stuck with him, and he with me. I could think of worse situations to be in.

But that also meant I needed to get him legal papers. As the arcane world continued to evolve in secret, I would have to hit up the Council of Witches for their assistance in sorting out his paperwork.

Not for the first time, I berated myself for not pursuing the craft more seriously. I didn't know anything about summoned demons. As I'd never been power hungry, I only dabbled in the lesser spells of convenience like the strength spell I used earlier this morning. Officially, I didn't belong to any coven, which left me in a rather vulnerable position and without some of the resources those more seriously involved benefited from.

Vazul's entrance into my life would require me to make a number of changes. More importantly, I would need to really sit down with him and sort out our future relationship. I was fine with a demon boyfriend, but I didn't want a slave. He called me

Mistress a few times, and that made me uncomfortable. We would figure out a way to cater to his need to perform tasks in a way that didn't make him a servant.

As if things were still steadily looking up, I quickly found a parking spot near the entrance and hurried inside. Having already pre-planned which stops I would make, I made a beeline for the main men's fashion store and grabbed the essentials. I should have questioned him about if he had specific preferences. Granted, I was only picking some undies, socks, a couple of pants, and shirts, but I didn't even know if he had color preferences. As his human form was also substantially bulkier than his demon one, I focused on buying items for the former. I suspected Vazul wouldn't bother with too many layers while at home in his natural form.

After picking up a pair of shoes, once again berating myself for not taking proper measurements, I headed for the checkout counters. I had just taken my credit card back from the cashier and was returning it to my wallet when a familiar voice resounded behind me.

"Fancy seeing you here!" Angelique said, with that annoying sultry voice she always used, thinking it made her sound seductive.

I groaned inwardly as I turned around to face her. I wasn't ready to have that confrontation so soon while still trying to sort out my own feelings about *my* demon. She glanced at the two heavy bags as the cashier placed the last shirt inside the left one. The speculative glimmer that sparked in her eyes, and the way they ever so slightly narrowed spelled trouble.

"Someone sure is on a shopping spree," Angelique said in the fakest enthusiastic voice. "Menswear at that! What's going on? Any news you'd like to share?"

I fought the urge to squirm, wondering how much or how little she knew. I doubted Sophia spilled the beans without my consent. As no one else would know, I could only pray that she was also clueless, and that she didn't remember she had left her egg in the apartment.

"Hey Angelique," I said politely. "I thought you were out of town."

She waved a dismissive hand. "I was. But I had to come back sooner to handle a big order. You know how impatient wealthy patrons can be."

"Right. So why didn't you drop by the apartment to fetch your stuff?" I asked, instantly flinching inwardly for raising the topic I wanted to avoid for now.

My wretched mouth would be my downfall. But I really wanted to call her out on her bullshit.

She gave me the least sincerely shocked expression before pressing her palm to her chest and looking at me apologetically.

"Oh shoot! I'm so sorry. It completely slipped my mind. I had so much going on."

"I bet. Well I got your stuff out to avoid Mrs. Hopkins charging us a cleaning fee."

"Aww, you're always so lovely!" she exclaimed in that patronizing fashion that systematically made me want to claw her pretty face and poke those baby blue eyes out. "I appreciate it. If you don't mind holding onto them for a few days, I'll arrange to have them picked up from your place."

"Sure, no problem."

I took the receipt from the cashier, tossed it into one of the bags, and picked them up, ready to leave.

"So you never told me who those clothes were for," Angelique said in a pretend friendly way, although I didn't miss the harder glint in her eyes implying that I wasn't going anywhere until I answered her questions.

"It's for my boyfriend," I said with a shrug.

Her eyes widened with genuine shock. "A boyfriend?! I didn't know you were dating anyone. Who is he?"

"No one you would know," I said in a non-committal fashion.

"Try me," she insisted.

"I assure you, it's no one you would know," I replied, lifting my chin slightly in a subtle act of defiance.

Anger flashed over her attractive face so quickly hidden most people would have missed it. But sharing an apartment with her for a year had taught me to recognize all the precursor signs of trouble. She flicked her long, platinum blonde hair over her shoulder as she gave me a greedy and speculative look.

Angie loved to steal other people's boyfriends. Anytime a woman in our circle of 'friends' expressed interest in a man, Angie would always swoop in and seduce him first. She had no interest in a long-term relationship with any of them. She only liked to brag that everyone else settled for her leftovers.

"Well then, that failure must be rectified. I *must* meet the man who has finally managed to capture the heart of our elusive little Coral!" she said with a sickly-sweet smile. "Make sure to bring him along to my party in two days."

"Your party?" I asked, confused.

"Oh! Did I forget to tell you?" she asked with that same fake innocence that made my skin crawl. "I'm holding a pre-fair party at my penthouse this Thursday."

"Wow! Then yeah, you totally forgot to invite me," I said in a neutral tone, although unsurprised.

Stupidly, it hurt my feelings not to have been invited, even though I actually disliked her and most of her inner circle. Chances were, I would have found an excuse not to attend. But it was the principle. I hated feeling excluded or unwanted, even by the likes of her. I seriously needed to cure myself of my people pleaser and pick me tendencies.

"Oh, my bad! But you must come. I'll have your favorite cocktail on hand as an apology and as a gesture of goodwill."

Your bad, my ass.

"I can't promise," I said in the same fake apologetic tone. "I still have a lot of final prep to do for the fair."

"I insist," she countered, in a tone that brooked no argument. "It would be unbecoming for you to be the only one not in attendance. I might think you're punishing me for accidentally forgetting to send you an invite," she added with an annoying pout that most people would find irresistibly cute.

"I'll do my best," I said with a stiff smile.

"See that you do," she replied with a big grin to soften the rudeness of her demand. "Tata!"

I cussed inwardly as I watched her strutting away, her ass swaying in an exaggerated fashion meant to draw every male's gaze, which she spectacularly succeeded at. But how could she not?

As obnoxious of an individual as she was, Mother Nature had been very generous to her. She was tall and statuesque. Her long, platinum hair fell to her behind. It wasn't her natural color, but you couldn't tell—not that she would ever admit to it. Her hourglass figure would have anyone drooling with envy. Her generous breasts were sheer perfection, big enough to draw attention, but not so much to imbalance her figure or risk falling into excessive territory. I highly suspected that a scalpel or two helped achieve that result. While her ass had nothing over mine, her legs were quite amazing.

Considering she was 5'10, it always confused me why she loved wearing crazy high stilettos. Granted, it made her long legs appear even more infinite and sexy. But I suspected it was just another way for her to dominate others.

Heaving a sigh, I turned around and made my way back to the car. If only I'd been here ten minutes sooner or later, I would have avoided the witch. The only reason she'd invited me was to test my boyfriend and see if she could lure him away before discarding him.

I simply won't go.

But I shut down that thought even as it popped into my mind. I couldn't avoid her forever. As Vazul would likely stick around for the long haul, them meeting was inevitable. The question was how much was I going to reveal when they did meet?

Whatever it was, I had two days to figure it out.

CHAPTER 5
VAZUL

I preened as Coral fawned over my work. Over the past two days, I'd been diligently fixing the many flaws in her designs. Most had been quite minor, but the obsessive-compulsive side of me simply couldn't leave it alone. Anyway, the ultimate result had been more than worth it.

What broke my brain was the constant guilt she felt about overworking me and her desire to find ways of rewarding and thanking me. My prior masters always exploited whatever I had to offer. Coral's lack of entitlement messed with my head. The annoying part was how often she tried to convince me to rest. She still struggled to understand that resting bored me to tears. It wasn't a reward but a punishment. And yet, her attentiveness to me was both refreshing and endearing.

I will not drain her.

Who would have thought the day would come when I would meet a master I actually wanted to keep permanently? And I truly wanted to keep her. Although I promised not to drain her, I could have used one of many workarounds to do it regardless. In fact, I considered it that first day and probably would have done so, had she been a foul Mistress.

When it came to toeing the line and finding loopholes, creatures of the underworld like me excelled at finding the cracks and slipping through them. In this instance, Coral made me promise not to drain her while we were intimate. She never mentioned any other moment. That made them fair game.

But I truly liked my little human. Therefore, in a few years, I would have to convince her to let me extend her lifespan indefinitely. I couldn't allow my Coral to age and die. I refused to even contemplate the horror of serving anyone other than her. She was perfect.

Her emotions tasted divine. I loved how she doted on me, took my wishes and needs into consideration, and possessed such a sweet and innocent soul. The most shocking part was how stellar sex with her was. As a Liderc, I always gave my partners the most mind-blowing experience. It was my duty. I rarely expected to receive in return and usually didn't. With her, it was different. She gave as much as she could, making certain my needs were tended to in all ways, be it sex or anything else.

The trip to the mall yesterday had been quite the riot. I was used to my masters simply dictating what I would wear and how I should behave. Most of the time, they demanded I dress in lurid fashions so that they could enjoy the view or flaunt me to their friends. Until now, it had never bothered me as it had been the norm. But with her, I was discovering something new.

My feelings mattered. I mattered. My desires mattered.

And above all, she was teaching me what it felt like to be treated with respect, kindness, and selfless generosity. She splurged on me to the point I had to tell her to stop it. What made it so amazing was the fact that she wasn't doing it to buy my loyalty or appreciation. Coral wanted me to be happy. Her emotions loudly broadcast that her sole concern was ensuring all my needs were met, and that I wasn't holding back out of some misplaced shyness or guilt at making her spend for me.

I didn't care how much money she spent. As her Liderc, it

was my duty to make sure she recovered it all and significantly increased her wealth thanks to my services.

As we walked through the mall, so many heads turned to admire the human form I had taken. He was an extremely handsome and muscular man, so people's reactions were unsurprising. The pride that radiated from her did the strangest thing to me. At first, I wondered if she would be offended by so many people drooling over her man. But it quickly became apparent that she loved that I drew so many eyes and especially that I ignored them all, focusing my attention on her instead.

The silly female didn't understand that no one could ever take me from her, even if I wanted to be—which I absolutely didn't.

Was it stupid that I hated that the entire world believed that my woman belonged to that human instead of me? I wanted to walk around in my demon form and shout from the rooftops that she was mine and I was hers. At least, Coral happily allowed me to stay in my true form at home. More importantly, not once had she requested or even wished for me to take a human appearance or a different face than my own during our intimate moments.

Most of the time, my masters demanded I remain in whatever human form they had chosen for me. After all, they didn't want me, Vazul. They just wanted the embodiment of the fantasy in their minds. It would hurt me deeply if my Coral suddenly started acting that way.

Obviously, I needed to get over it. So long as we lived in the Mortal Realm, I would never be able to show my true face by her side in public, except maybe during All Hallows. The question that plagued me was whether this would last. I loved her happy emotions and how she responded to me. The thought that she might tire of me and want to move on was devastating. We'd only just met, but I was already hooked.

And tonight would be the real test.

I had a bad feeling about Angie's party. Watching my woman

fidget and stress out for two days since receiving the invitation both amused and irked me. Obviously, Angelique would want me—who wouldn't? But that was too damn bad for her. My silly Mistress still struggled to comprehend that she fully owned me, not only through our magic bond, but also because I chose to remain hers.

No matter. It would all become clear soon enough.

As we settled in her car—me in the passenger seat—I put on my seat belt with a pout. Coral gave me a confused look when I crossed my arms over my chest and stared forward. I was being ridiculous, but I couldn't help feeling annoyed.

"What's wrong?" Coral asked carefully.

"I'm your Liderc. I should be driving you to your destination as you enjoy the view, not be chauffeured around by you. I hate feeling useless," I grumbled.

She gaped at me for a second before chuckling. That she found my reaction silly—valid though her response was—aggravated me a bit more. Yet, the amused and slightly tender emotions emanating from her mollified me. I fucking loved her sweeter emotions.

"Vazul, you're so stinking adorable," she said softly. "You're not being useless. You're keeping me company and being my mental support during an evening I really don't want to attend. Anyway, you can't drive until we have sorted out your papers. But don't worry, soon enough you'll be the one complaining about how much driving I'm making you do."

"It will never be too much," I countered firmly with a haughty sniff.

She chuckled again and took off. It was a twenty-minute drive to our destination—a fancy housing complex located near the heart of downtown. During the journey, Coral gave me a quick breakdown of the people who would be in attendance, and the things to watch out for. Her nervousness when it came to

Angelique was almost palpable. It shamed me to admit that her fear of losing me tickled me pink.

We entered the building and made our way to the elevators. It flew up to one of the penthouses. The closer we got to our destination, the more restless my Mistress became. It displeased me tremendously. At first, I egotistically assumed it was all due to her apprehension about Angie's reaction to me. But it finally dawned on me that it was the entire circle that made her uneasy. She didn't want to be with these people.

So why are we here?

I almost suggested that we leave but kept my peace. In the end, the situation with Angie needed to be put to rest. Delaying things wouldn't do us any good. And I wouldn't tolerate my Coral's delicious emotions being tainted by this type of stress.

The most intense sense of déjà vu slapped me the moment the door opened before us. So many times before, in far older eras, I had attended this type of gathering. It was always the same thing. Most of the guests possessed varying levels of magic, with only a handful of others being laymen, mundane, or normies—as non-magic users were often referred as.

It always baffled me why these people congregated together. Half of them disliked each other—not to say flat out despised— and would stomp all over each other to get ahead. Most harbored some sort of jealousy or envy hidden behind syrupy smiles and backhanded compliments. They were fully aware that beneath those fake friendships, they were all using each other either as steppingstones to increase their power, or as punching bags to make themselves feel superior. No wonder my Coral didn't want to be a part of this. Her soul was too sweet and pure for these jackals.

To be fair, not all of them were foul. In fact, Sophia turned out to be quite pleasant. Like the others, she only mingled with this group in order to increase her power. But she did so while earning everything through hard work instead of trying to leech off others. She understood that you couldn't grow in this field by isolating yourself, like my Mistress was. Sophia just excelled at navigating safely in a shark-infested sea.

Obviously, I had known Coral's magic to be fairly basic. But now, standing amidst her peers, I realized that she was barely a novice, a baby amongst powerful witches. It whipped all of my protective instincts into a frenzy. However powerful these witches were, none compared to me. Anyone who tried to mess with my Mistress would find out the hard way.

"Coral, there you are!" said an attractive female with an excessive enthusiasm as she pushed her way through the crowd and headed towards us.

A single glance sufficed for me to know this was Angelique. The long silver white hair alone gave it away. Her ankle-length, second skin of a black dress left little to the imagination. The plunging neckline was deep enough to give vertigo to the most resilient person. And yet, she managed to make it look elegant instead of vulgar. How she managed to walk on those sky-high stilettos defied gravity. The blood red lipstick on her generous lips certainly served its purpose in drawing attention to her face.

Every man in attendance couldn't help but steal covetous glances her way, even those whose emotions claimed they resented and even hated her.

"And what a mighty fine specimen of manhood you have brought us tonight," Angie continued, pressing her hand to her chest.

The same blood-red color on her manicured nails acted in a similar fashion as they did on her lips, but this time by drawing wandering eyes to her perky breasts.

"No wonder you kept him hidden from us. In your shoes, I'd definitely do the same."

She added that last sentence while giving me a less-than-subtle once over.

"Hello, Angelique," Coral replied with the appropriate level of friendliness, even though every emotion radiating from her expressed that she wanted to cuss her out instead. "Thank you for the invitation. This is my *boyfriend*, Vazul Droog. Vazul, please meet our host, Angelique Delaney."

Droog wasn't my last name. Lidercs—and most underworld beings for that matter—didn't have surnames. But in the Mortal Realm, we often took a last name that represented the circle we came from, our breed, or classification. In my case, it was an anagram of the Hungarian word Ördög, which meant demon.

Despite knowing she intended to introduce me that way, Coral claiming me as her boyfriend instead of her servant did the craziest thing to me. The not-so-subtle way in which she emphasized the nature of our relationship almost made me hard. I loved being publicly claimed by her. I wanted to thump my chest and shout from the rooftops. Instead, I slipped a possessive arm around my woman, drew her tightly against me, and settled my palm just on the side of that scrumptious behind of hers.

Fuck, now I want to give it a good nip again!

"Hello, Ms. Delaney," I said in my most courteous voice.

We had never met, and yet I recognized the unpleasant taste of her emotions. I remembered all too well the time she devoted trying to get me to hatch. The greed, the impatience, the anger, and the malice had been overwhelming. She'd acquired my egg with very specific goals in mind. My failure to hatch on her timeline infuriated her as it derailed the lucrative plans she had been setting in motion. Once she realized who I was, she would lose her shit.

And I was here for it.

"Oh please, call me Angelique, or better yet, just Angie!" she exclaimed with an almost offended expression. "Ms. Delaney is my mother. I'm much too young and single to be called this way in an intimate setting, and especially among friends. So I hope you'll allow me to call you Vazul. Such a lovely and unusual name."

I responded with a stiff smile and bowed my head in concession. Although she couldn't find fault with my response, the perceptive female immediately caught that her charms weren't working on me. The instant anger that stirred within her pleased me to no end.

And we're only getting started.

"But do come in," she continued, gesturing at the interior of the impressively large penthouse.

To my utter annoyance, she seized the opportunity to touch my bare upper arm, giving it a shameless caress while pretending to be nudging me forward. I pulled away from her touch in a way that wasn't flat out rude but also left little doubt that I did not appreciate the contact.

She licked her lips, her wheels spinning as to how she was going to get me to give in to her. Far from offending her, my reaction only made her even more determined to have her way. To Angelique, my resistance wasn't sincere. The wretched female believed I was merely playing hard to get and issuing a direct challenge to what she deemed herself entitled to.

I couldn't wait to crush her spirit a bit more with each of her disrespectful attempts.

"Everyone, this is the very handsome Vazul, gracing us with his presence. Please see to it that you make him feel very welcome," Angelique shouted to all the attendees.

Like properly trained pets, most of them approached us, giving a polite greeting to Coral before excessively fussing over me. Saying I wanted to crack each and every one of their skulls would be quite the understatement.

The only thing that made it bearable was how relieved my Mistress felt about having less focus on her. The guilt she felt about me sustaining the brunt of all that unrequited attention might have been problematic. But it soon gave way to almost malicious enjoyment as she watched me squash every overly flirtatious overture the other guests made me. It was obvious enough to recognize it for what it was, but also not so blatant that you could openly call them out for it.

Merely moments after I finally finished being introduced to all the attendees, Angie invited everyone to follow her to her workshop for an exclusive preview of her collection. I frowned when Coral instantly tensed. Why would she be so worried? I didn't know what Angie might have concocted, but my Mistress' collection was absolutely stellar. By the time I finished polishing what she had already put together, it would be very hard to rival.

With a theatrical gesture, our hostess opened wide the double doors located at the other end of the penthouse. As one, the crowd started moving forward. We followed, lagging a bit behind as I took in our surroundings.

The place was flawless in a very clinical and calculated way. Everything was in shades of dark blues, black, deep burgundy, and little hints of silver. That latter color surprised me. I would have expected gold instead. The clever balancing of so many dark colors with white ceilings and much lighter furniture kept the place from being gloomy. The countless immense windows also made the place more luminous. During the daytime, it had to be wonderful. And the evening was nothing to sneeze at either, as it offered a breathtaking view of the illuminated city at night.

However, this entire place had no soul. The modern furniture with sharp edges and polished surfaces didn't beckon you to just sit down and relax. You constantly felt like you had to check yourself not to break anything like in a showroom. We might as well have been transported into one of those interior decorating magazines. Chances were that was exactly where this entire design came from.

In sharp contrast, my Coral's house boasted warm earthy tones, with lots of beige, cream, and little blasts of color that made it inviting. But above all, her decor had personality to it and said something about her. Whether some quirky mask on the wall, exotic sculpture on her shelf, or various literature from over-the-top comedy to very serious encyclopedias, with the occasional murder mystery and even comic book, everything revealed one of the many mesmerizing facets of who she was.

As soon as we entered the workshop, the stench of imp magic slapped my nose. I couldn't repress a snort as I approached the rather impressive collection. Coral peered up at me with curiosity and more of that nonsensical insecurity. The silly female thought that my reaction might have been prompted by the fact that I was blown away by her rival's collection—although Angelique clearly was no competition.

I gave her a reassuring smile laced with smugness that had her eyes widen in surprise. She didn't know what thoughts were coursing through my mind, but the way her shoulders relaxed indicated she at least understood that my thoughts were positive on her behalf. I couldn't wait to get back in the car and tell her why she should pat herself on the back.

The collection was as well executed as it was unimaginative. Where my Coral had created her own story of a haunting wreaking havoc on the Victorian city, Angie had fallen back on a safe classic. Her collection revolved around the story of Dracula. Every building and outdoors scene featured key moments of the tale. Although she also had a variety of miniature items as stand-alones, she didn't have the furniture with embedded miniature inserts.

I highly doubted anyone else would, aside from maybe some book nooks.

While I couldn't fault Angie for not necessarily possessing the storytelling talent that my woman did, it was the fact that she hadn't performed the work herself that irked me. Did she even possess any crafting abilities? Because she clearly had not done any of this work. I could almost see the residual magic that had woven these objects into existence. My Coral had done all the work herself, and I had just stepped in to polish it. Granted, there were no rules requiring that the exhibitors do all the manual labor themselves, but it underlined how my female was the superior miniaturist.

I struggled not to roll my eyes as Angelique strutted her stuff and preened under the praises people were showering her with. We also politely complimented her on her collection. It wasn't even a lie to the extent that it was indeed decent. It just didn't live up to my woman's work—not that I was biased in any way.

But as we reconvened into the living area, the other guests constantly appeared to have a reason to try and lure Coral away to discuss something in private. By pure *coincidence* no doubt, Angie always conveniently happened to be lurking nearby and strolling over to strike a conversation with me. Avoiding her was becoming a most infuriating challenge.

At one point, when Myrtil, the Head Priestess of Angelique's coven requested a word with my woman, I nearly snapped. This time, she didn't just take her a few steps away just out of hearing distance. Myrtil flat out dragged Coral onto the immense terrace and closed the glass doors behind them.

I didn't even have to look to feel our hostess barreling down on me from behind. The gleeful, predatory emotions radiating from her shouted her intentions loud and clear. Pretending not to be aware of her approach, I headed towards the bar with all the refreshments to get myself a drink and a second one for my Mistress. Before I could even grab a glass, Angie bumped into me, acting as if she'd lost her footing.

"Oh dear! I'm so sorry!" she exclaimed, clinging to me as if for dear life. "You'd think I'd be less clumsy walking in these heels. After all, I've pounded many catwalks on even higher heels than these ones."

She added that last part while straightening and lifting her leg to show me. Naturally, it was the leg on the side of the insanely high slit of her skirt. The silky fabric of her black dress slipped sideways, showing the flawless skin of her slender thigh all the way down to her feet.

"Maybe you should change into something less challenging then," I said in a neutral voice while gently but firmly removing her hands from me.

"And ruined my attire?" she asked, eyes wide with fake innocence and surprise. "Impossible. Those shoes are perfect with this outfit," she added, running her hands down her sides in a caress that highlighted the curves of her body.

"Then make sure you are more careful. It would be unfortunate to be stuck with a twisted ankle right before a major exhibit," I said with a cold smile.

"Unfortunate indeed," she said, trying to hide her irritation with my distant behavior. "How come I've never seen you before? I pride myself to know every remarkable and influential individual in this city. How come I've never run into you before? Such a handsome man would be heavily talked about among the fairer sex. How did Coral snag you under our collective noses?"

"Coral didn't snag *me*. *I* snagged her. The moment I became aware of her, I knew she had to be mine, and I had to be hers. So I came to her and refused to take no for an answer until she honored me by claiming me as hers," I said with a smile, my eyes locked with hers.

She scrunched her face as if she had bitten into something sour before quickly regaining her composure.

"Wow. That's quite unexpected."

"Is that so?" I challenged, raising an inquisitive eyebrow.

"Well yes. Coral is a very sweet and charming young woman. But she's such a quiet homebody, I would have expected a man like you to be more into wilder and stronger women, with a fierce appetite for all the thrills life has to offer," she said resting her palm on top of the table as she leaned slightly forward, giving me a better glimpse of her chest.

To her dismay, I didn't glance down at her cleavage, but kept my eyes locked with hers.

"First, being quiet and finding fulfillment in a home you love does not make one boring or weak. Ever heard of quiet strength? You don't have to be loud to be powerful. In fact, it's the quiet ones you should always beware of. You never know what secrets they keep and just how great their hand is until they finally choose to lay down their cards. Do not underestimate my woman."

She huffed. "While I agree with your statement in principle, you may not know that I shared an apartment with Coral for a year. She's a sweet girl, predictable, and a completely open book. There is no powerful secret. We would know…"

"You can be married to someone for twenty years only to realize you actually never really knew them. Do not presume to know Coral," I replied dismissively. "Which leads me to the second point. We've only just met, and yet you think you know what kind of man I am. What would that be, exactly?"

The way she perked up at that question indicated she'd been looking for that very opening to launch her attack.

"I do not need to know you for long to understand that you are an apex alpha," Angelique said in a purring tone. "You are strong, a leader of men. Your mere presence commands attention. That impressive body of yours screams of discipline and dedication. One doesn't get this lean and muscular without having a healthy and steady routine. The way you present yourself from your clothes, your hair, the subtle yet alluring aroma of your cologne speaks of elegance, refinement, and impeccable taste. And beneath that delicious package, a lion prowls, ready to devour its prey. And I can assure you, any prey you set your sights on would be a willing sacrifice."

She added that last sentence leaning forward, her lips parted as if inviting me to kiss her.

I stared at her for a second, letting the tension build in

tandem with her ridiculous expectations. Then I snorted and shook my head while looking at her with disbelief. She stiffened, shocked and offended by my response.

"That's a very interesting take. I want to believe that people would indeed consider me a leader, not that I particularly care or seek anyone's approval. As for my body, I'm actually what one would call a slacker when it comes to fitness training. I just happened to have an exceptional metabolism. And regarding my fashion sense, you should congratulate my woman instead as all of these were chosen by her for me," I said as I tauntingly waved at my body. "Her taste in everything is always impeccable."

"Oh, stop playing coy," she snapped, sounding a little irritated. "Why settle when you can have so much more? A man like you could have anything, and *anyone*."

This time, my gaze hardened. "I'm not playing coy. And frankly, your words would be flattering if you weren't being so disrespectful to my woman right now."

"Stop calling her *your woman*!" she hissed. "You deserve much more than that mousey little girl. Let me help you see reason."

To my shock, she waved her hand and whispered an incantation in such a low voice that most humans wouldn't have heard it, or it would have sounded like nothing more than a sigh. But the wretched female had cast a love spell on me. Confident in my inability to resist, Angie leaned forwards as she caressed my biceps left exposed by the short-sleeved shirt I was wearing. She clearly intended to press her chest against mine and maybe even embrace me, but the foolish female was messing with the wrong male.

With a single thought, I ignited my fire beneath the skin of my upper arm. The lightning-shaped fiery tendrils flared at one of the intense heat levels I normally used for defense in combat. Angie immediately yelped and yanked her hand away from me as she stumbled a couple of steps back. Holding the wrist of her wounded hand, she stared at the latter in horror. An angry red welt was already swelling in the middle of her palm. Angie glanced back at me, shock, confusion, and a hint of fear flashing in quick succession on her face.

"Please, you foolish woman. Your pathetic lust spells do not work on the likes of me. Shame on you for trying to steal the partner of someone you claim to be your friend. And even greater shame on you for trying to coerce someone into noncon-sensual frolic. I doubt the Council of Witches would approve."

She paled and took a step back while holding her injured hand against her chest.

"What are you?" she whispered, fear and confusion audible in her voice.

I stared at her quietly for a moment, then put down the glass I had initially picked up without bothering to fill it, then started walking away. She immediately recited an incantation. It repre-sented no threat to me. But it also meant the gig was up.

"Oh, my God! You're a Liderc!" she exclaimed.

A few people peered at us. They hadn't understood what she had said thanks to the ambient music providing a semblance of privacy, and the fact that everyone had conveniently stayed out of hearing range as soon as their dear hostess had cornered me. A single vicious glare from Angie sufficed for them to avert their eyes.

I stopped and turned back to face her. She stared at me in disbelief, her mind struggling to reconcile this impossible reality.

"How in the world did Coral of all people manage to get…?"

Angelique's voice trailed off as her brain finally put two and two together. At that moment, I realized that she had truly forgotten that she left my egg lying around, discarded in her old apartment.

"Oh, my God! You're mine! That bitch stole you from me!" she hissed, anger twisting her features in a rather unattractive fashion.

"Careful how you address my woman," I warned, taking a menacing step forward. "Coral stole nothing from you."

"You came from *my* egg," she snarled, slapping her chest with her good hand. "I paid a fortune to acquire you!"

"And then you discarded the egg. You abandoned it in your former apartment, and it would have been trashed if not for my woman retrieving it. Therefore, you have no claim. Owning an egg means nothing. It is the one who hatches it who holds every right."

"And that was me!" she exclaimed angrily, advancing another step. "For three months, I incubated you. It was I who did all the work."

I shrugged. "Clearly, you did it wrong. It doesn't take that long to hatch one of us."

"Right or wrong, you're still mine," she said with a dismissive gesture before giving me a baffled look. "Why do you want her anyway? She's the weakest witch I've ever met—if she can even be called that. She's boring and probably insanely vanilla in bed. She will cramp your style with her stiff, prim and proper ways. You'll be begging to be freed of her before the week ends."

The expression on my face must have made it clear she had better tread carefully as I would not tolerate her continued disrespect of my Mistress. Switching up tactics, she shed all angry or aggressive demeanor and returned to the enticing seductress she'd initially greeted me with.

"I can give you the life of endless lust one such as you crave. With me, no kink, no form of debauchery will be off limits. There will be no feeding restrictions, which I'm sure Coral has imposed on you. We both know that she will keep you from exploring your sensuality with anyone else. Whereas I will happily share all that you have to offer with others. My friends will gladly give up some of their lifeforce to feed and sustain you as part of the most potent sex rituals. What more could a sex demon possibly want? You name it, and it's yours. All you have to do is come back to your rightful owner."

I shook my head at her with a bored expression. "While all of this might have been tempting to another, it does not appeal to me in any way. Do not waste your time—and especially mine— arguing with me. Whatever you can offer is irrelevant. I belong to Coral, forever. Now, if you'll excuse me, I would like to spend the evening with my woman."

I turned around and left.

"We shall see about that," Angelique hissed behind my back in an angry whisper.

The murderous rage radiating from her made it clear she meant every word. This woman would seek to make our lives miserable. But she would soon discover I wasn't one to be played with. Whatever she had in store for us, I'd be ready. And then, I'd make her rue the day she ever attempted to cross my Mistress.

CHAPTER 6
CORAL

After Myrtil hogged me for nearly half an hour, I could have wept with relief when Vazul barged in on our conversation and expressed his desire to leave. I didn't even ask him the reason why and jumped at the opportunity to get the heck out of there.

It shamed me to admit that the entire time I feared I would lose him tonight. With everyone multiplying the ways to drag me away from him, it didn't take a genius to understand they were playing wingman to Angie. I didn't understand this blind loyalty, especially since so many of them disliked her.

Sophia actually intervened a few times, injecting herself in the conversation to free me from a particularly clingy minion keeping me from my man. I loved her for it. Although I wished she could have done more, my friend was walking on thin ice. As a member of Angelique's coven, Sophia had to tread carefully not to be too obvious in her efforts to assist me for fear she might become a pariah herself. While we got along great and genuinely appreciated each other, we weren't so close that she would jeopardize the future she'd been working so hard for to protect me. Anyway, I didn't want that for her either. I was just grateful for whatever assistance I could get.

However, the biggest shock came from Myrtil. As the Head Priestess of their coven, she should be setting the example instead of enabling one of her witches who was attempting to cause harm or distress to another. Granted, I wasn't officially a member of their coven. But I was still 'friends' with all of them. After all, the only reason I hadn't joined their rank was my lack of assiduity in my training. The door was open to me, but I had to reach the basic requirement level. But even with that, if only for ethical reasons, Myrtil shouldn't have allowed herself to become an accomplice.

The most infuriating part was that I couldn't even openly accuse her of plotting with Angie against me. The conversation had been similar to the ones she and I had in the past regarding my lack of commitment to magical training. According to her, I possessed great potential that I was allowing to go to waste.

And she was right. Magic came easily to me. With a bit of focus and regular training, I truly believed I could surpass Angelique. However, I couldn't picture myself interacting on a regular basis with this crowd. I didn't trust any of them. So having them as mentors felt a little suicidal to me. I wouldn't put it past a few of them to cause genuine harm out of jealousy under the guise of pranks or hazing.

As I drove us back home, I stole many wary glances at Vazul. He was sitting quietly, staring straight ahead, the barely visible crease on his forehead indicating that he was intensely reflecting on something. Unable to stand the silence any longer, I took a deep breath and then went for it.

"I'm sorry for what my friends put you through," I said in an apologetic tone.

He gave me a sideways look, his expression hinting that I had just said something ludicrous.

"Don't be. You're not responsible for their actions. And do

not call them your friends. None of them are, except for Sophia," he said in a factual manner.

I flinched. I now understood that Vazul unintentionally spoke in a way that sometimes came across as cruel and insensitive. It was comparable to the way one occasionally blurted out something they shouldn't have then immediately kicked themselves for it. However, there was no self-kicking where my demon was concerned as he didn't see how his words were harmful. He was merely being honest and stating facts, not opinions.

This cut deep simply because I knew it to be true. But the people pleaser in me kept clinging to hope that some way, somehow, they would eventually recognize my worth as a person and as a friend.

"Why do you mingle with these people?" he asked in a soft tone with genuine curiosity and confusion.

I shifted uneasily in the driver's seat and took a moment to reflect on my answer.

"I don't really hang out with any of them anymore, except with Sophia from time to time. Angie and I attended the same Fine Arts program in college. I focused on sculpture and woodworking while she focused on painting. But we both partook in miniature art workshops. That's how we started talking."

He nodded with an unimpressed expression that took me aback at first.

"Right. And let me guess, many of those conversations revolved around her gleaning ideas from you?"

Even though he formulated it as a question, it was more of a statement. I snorted, blown away by his intuition. Or was it his ability to read people?

"It took me too long to realize that she was indeed fishing for ideas she could appropriate. Sadly, I've struggled my whole life with pretty bad people-pleasing tendencies," I conceded with self-derision. "But being approached by the popular girl flattered my ego. It turned out she and her roommate were looking for a third to replace the one who had just left. Sharing an apartment would allow me to save even more money towards the downpayment for my house and starting my own business. So yeah, I jumped at the opportunity."

"How convenient," he replied.

"More like how unsurprising. It wasn't until I moved in that I realized how unbearable living with her was. But that's also how I met Sophia. She and I immediately clicked. Even though we have very different personalities. She's Teflon, where I'm a doormat. She comes in, does what she needs to do regardless of how toxic and unpleasant the situation is, then walks out and washes it off totally unscathed. I just get stuck with everyone else's dirt sinking into every fiber of my being."

"You're not a doormat," he said sternly. "You're an empath. And people take advantage of it. We'll just need to work on you setting and enforcing your boundaries. But fear not. You have me now to remind you and run interference until you own the inner strength I see clearly in you."

My chest warmed for my demon. If I hadn't been driving right now, I would have given him a bone crushing hug.

"You're giving me whiplash," I mumbled to hide my embarrassment.

"Whiplash?" Vazul asked, slightly confused.

"You can be such a jerk sometimes with your brutal bluntness. And then, you turn around and say something so incredibly sweet."

He gave me an odd look before shrugging. "In all instances, I'm merely speaking the truth as I see it. It is *you* misinterpreting my intentions as being a jerk. Whatever my actions or words, know that where you are concerned, they will never be fueled by malice or cruelty. I exist to improve your life and make you thrive."

"Like I said, whiplash…" I repeated, while melting from the inside out.

He snorted.

"Anyway, it was Sophia who got me into magic. I didn't even know it was a real thing," I continued. "Angie only invited me to share their apartment because she could feel my latent talent. It also made it easier for her to have unfettered access to my ideas so that she could appropriate them."

"Naturally," he replied, his voice thick with sarcasm. "But she seems quite wealthy. Why did she need roommates?"

"Because we had a fancy apartment on campus. Sadly for her, that specific one required three people. Once their former roommate left, they needed a replacement or they would have had to relinquish the place and downgrade. It's far more convenient to live on campus rather than deal with the nightmare traffic every day."

"Then I'll just rejoice that you had to deal with it long enough to hatch me," he said teasingly.

I snorted and playfully elbowed him. Still, it gave me warm fuzzies whenever he spoke like that.

"I guess it wasn't such a bad thing after all, despite what an aggravating experience it had been," I concurred.

"So how come you're not part of their coven?" he asked, genuinely intrigued.

"Honestly, I considered it. In fact, I really enjoyed discovering all the things that I could do with it. Magic is really cool. The camaraderie of a coven also appealed to me as I'd often felt like the odd girl out who didn't really fit in any particular group. Even Myrtil, the Head Priestess, said I had great potential. But that entire crowd makes me feel uneasy."

"Of course," he replied in a self-evident manner. "They have very different values, morals, and ambitions. You are a sheep among wolves with them."

That stung. Although I understood he hadn't meant it in a derogatory way, it still made me feel less, and like the pushover I too often tended to be.

"You must find me boring in comparison," I said, immediately mentally kicking myself for sounding so pathetic and needy.

"Don't be silly," he said with a frown. "If you weren't currently driving us—which I should be doing—I'd put you across my knees and give you a proper spanking. And not of the fun type. Everything about you tastes and feels better than those sharks. Stop comparing yourself with people who are inferior to you in all the ways that matter. Their magic means nothing. With proper training, you will by far exceed theirs. But no amount of effort or even therapy will make them emotionally even half as wonderful as you are. I'm glad you hatched me instead of her. I would never want to belong to any of them while I happily belong to you."

Yep, my ovaries exploded again. It was a miracle I didn't crash into some wall or run a red light as I was so busy flying high under his sweet words.

"See! The emotions you currently feel taste divine. Stop ruining my snacks with irrational and unfounded feelings," he grumbled.

The silliest grin stretched my lips as I beamed at him.

"Then just keep being this sweet to me, and I'll continue to feel emotions that are tasty to you," I deadpanned.

"Challenge accepted," he said in a slightly menacing tone that had me tingling in all the right places.

Needless to say that as soon as we got home, I properly thanked him in the naughtiest fashion.

The next morning, I was examining my standard size coffee table showstopper. I'd spent an insane amount of time building the intricately carved, wooden table, leaving the interior hollow so that I could embed an alchemist lab. However, I built an alternate miniature insert so that people could see the endless customization options. And I fell madly in love with the haunted Victorian street option instead.

The result exceeded all my expectations, especially after Vazul worked his magic, polishing the elements I hadn't done as flawlessly as they could have been, or by replacing certain materials to heighten the realism.

I had just finished setting up the electrical elements of the miniature. It allowed windows to light up automatically at night. The timer also included a randomizer so that not all windows would turn on or off at the same time, creating the illusion that real people on varied schedules inhabited that street. That worked perfectly, as did the lighting up the 'gas' lamp posts lining the street. However, as I stood there chewing my bottom lip, I pondered about adding the occasional flicker to one or two of them. But this would require additional electrical work that I didn't think was worth the hassle or the risk involved, especially so close to the deadline.

"Stop chewing your mouth. That's my job," Vazul grumbled before pulling on my bottom lip.

I snorted and made a face at him.

"I'm thinking," I said.

"Well think with your head, not with your mouth. What are you torturing yourself over this time?" he asked.

"I'm debating whether it's worth adding a flicker to some of the lamp posts or devote time to adding some fog on the ground," I said pensively. "The flicker wouldn't be that complicated, but every electrical component only increases the risks of some random malfunction at the worst possible time. As for the fog, in order for the owner to be able to trigger it at will, I would need some built in humidifier. But that could cause mold or other issues in the long run, especially with the electrical components for the lights."

"Then use magic," Vazul countered in a self-evident manner.

"There are plenty of low-level spells that can create those illusions. Just place invisible runes activated by basic words of power. People won't even need magic to make them work. To them, it will be no different than any other voice-activated equipment that they have. You could even have ghostly figures crossing the street or appearing in random places once night falls."

My eyes widened, and I stared at him in shock to have him describe exactly the thing I wished I could have added but crossed out of my realistic accomplishment list.

He chuckled. "Stop being so shocked. I can see what you want. How do you think I managed to polish your creations exactly to your vision? Just add them. It will make your masterpiece complete."

"But I don't know those spells," I said sheepishly.

"Then learn them," he snarled, unimpressed. "There are very basic spells that you can master in a couple of hours."

"Is that even ethical?" I asked, shifting uneasily on my feet.

He huffed. "Angelique's collection is entirely built using magic, and not even her own. If that was a problem, she would have been called out for it a long time ago. At the end of the day, the only rules are that you own all the rights to your collection, that they meet the basic quality levels, and that they are safe for the public. You meet all of those requirements. So get going."

I started chewing my bottom lip again, my nerves getting the best of me as my back tensed. He was right. They were the type of low-level spells that I could easily master if I put my mind to it. But I was feeling overwhelmed at the thought of everything I wanted to do with the clock ticking.

I yelped when Vazul suddenly pressed his chest against my back and slipped a hand under the waistband of my skirt. His fingers immediately went for my clit and started rubbing it.

"What are you doing?!" I exclaimed, even as a bolt of lust exploded in the pit of my stomach.

"You stress too much over minor things. I'm helping you relax," he said nonchalantly.

"You can't do that!"

"Obviously, I can," he deadpanned, two fingers dipping inside of me as his thumb continued to massage my clit. He snuck his left hand under my shirt to grab my breast. "And clearly, I am."

"Clearly. But how am I supposed to focus?" I said in a disapproving tone belied by my legs spreading with a will of their own to give him better access.

"You figure it out. It is your job to do the thinking. Mine is doing. And right now, I want to do *you*," he purred before brushing his fangs over the side of my neck.

"Vazul!" I protested in the weakest and most pathetic way, my inner walls throbbing in anticipation.

The sound of the doorbell ringing nearly had me jumping out of my skin. The string of curse words that tumbled out of my demon's mouth echoed the ones racing through my mind. Who the hell wanted to be disturbed by a random visitor just when they were getting fingered by their sex demon, who would soon thereafter fuck them to oblivion?

With much reluctance, I freed myself of my lover's naughty touch, adjusted my clothes, and headed out of the room. It suddenly struck me that it was likely the delivery of the additional material I ordered at the last minute. I would get those in the house quickly before rushing back to Vazul so that he could properly wreck me.

My cheeks wanted to burn with embarrassment that I should have turned into such a sex starved maniac since he entered my life. But you only lived once. Not enjoying my Liderc to the fullest extent would not only be a crime against humanity but would also make me a dreadful Mistress. After all, he'd only recently hatched and needed to be properly fed. Who was I to deny him such basic needs?

I cackled softly at the shamelessness with which I tried to justify embracing the inner tramp that I'd stupidly repressed for far too long.

No, not repressed. It hadn't found the right partner to be able to be set free.

That sudden realization struck me hard. I wasn't just acting up because some freaky underworld being had entered my life. I was finally letting my guard down and exploring the part of me that I never would have exposed to others before. Not because there was anything wrong with it, but because I never would have felt as safe with anyone other than with my demon. I couldn't read emotions the way he did, and yet I knew beyond the shadow of a doubt that he never judged me or condemned any thought or desire I might have.

He accepted me just the way I was. That he pushed me to work on my shortcomings wasn't a negative judgment about me. As he himself said, Vazul wanted me to achieve my full potential, and that required some work.

With him, I felt like even the sky wasn't the limit. So long as I put my heart into it, I could achieve my goals with him always standing by, ready to catch me should I ever stumble along the way.

I sauntered to the front door with a wistful smile on my face, only to have it wiped out the minute I opened the door.

"Angie?! What are you doing here?" I asked, distraught by the sight of the unpleasant female.

"I came to get what's mine," she said in a commanding tone, before pushing past me and barging inside the house.

Shocked, I gasped at the entitlement and rudeness. I was opening my mouth to give her a piece of my mind when my gaze landed on her bags still piled up next to the console in the entrance hall. Although I knew the real motive for her presence, I decided to play the game and see where it would lead us.

"Sure, your bags are all right here," I said, pointing at them.

She scoffed at them before turning back to glare at me.

"Don't play dumb," she snapped. "No one cares about that trash. I want my Liderc, you thief!"

I lifted my chin defiantly. "We both know I didn't steal anything. He's not yours. *You* didn't hatch him. *I* did. Therefore, you have no claim over him."

"You stole my property!" she snarled.

"You discarded the egg. That item became fair game."

"I left it to be retrieved later along with my other stuff," Angelique countered. "You said yourself to come get my stuff whenever. Well, whenever is right now."

"I did," I conceded. "And your stuff is all sitting right there. Except, by your own words, it is trash that no one cares about."

"The egg—"

"The egg is no more," I interrupted in a harsh tone. "It has hatched, and the shell has disintegrated. Now, a full sentient person exists. There is no object or property for you to claim."

"Vazul is not a person. He's a demon, a servant. MY servant," Angelique hissed. "You cannot fulfill his needs like I can. I bet you don't even feed him properly because you're too pathetic to allow him to drain a sliver of your lifeforce."

That comment struck a nerve. Even though Vazul promised that feeding off my emotions without leeching me was enough to sustain him, I couldn't help but wonder if he was just saying that to please me or if he was actually growing weaker by the day for lack of proper sustenance. Something on my face must have given away that she had guessed right as a look of malicious triumph sparked in her blue eyes.

"I knew it. You're so fucking weak, and you think you can own someone like him?" she gloated, taking a menacing step towards me. "I can ruin you, little girl. I have money, connections, and the law on my side. You are currently causing me severe financial harm."

I recoiled, flabbergasted by that insane accusation.

"Financial harm?! How the hell am I hurting you?"

"The egg cost a fortune," Angelique said smugly. "The price is high enough to qualify as grand larceny, an indictable offense. Added to that, *my* Liderc's labor would not only offset that initial investment, but it would also help generate considerable long-term revenue for me. You are depriving me of this. For months now, I've had many clients lined up to benefit from his services."

My jaw dropped. "So you want to pimp him out?!"

It was her turn to lift her chin defiantly, daring me to challenge both her right and the wisdom of her approach.

"How many men and women do you know who wouldn't be willing to pay a fortune for the privilege of safely fucking a demon?" she asked, greed shining bright in her eyes.

"Oh, my God! You mean to *literally* pimp him out, *sexually*, not just his *labor*!" I exclaimed, completely floored even as anger swelled within me. "That is absolutely out of the question. Vazul is not some prostitute for you to exploit!"

"He's a sex demon, you stupid cunt! Fucking is what he does. I can assure you that he wants that far more than the lame ass chores you're probably giving him. You cannot give him what he wants or needs. What in the world ever made you think that someone like you could hold on to an otherworldly creature like him?"

Each of her words felt like a searing dagger stabbing me in the heart, exposing each of the fears that kept swirling inside my head. He was a sex demon. Why would he be content with me when he could have anyone he desired and indulge in the more extreme kinks I would never be into?

Angelique's anger suddenly faded, and she took on an air of pity mixed with benevolence that hurt even more.

"I get it. I'm sure your pussy has never had it so good. After all, it's not like the top men were knocking down your door. So I can be lenient. After you return my property, I'll let him fuck you once a week for free. That'll be far more action—and prime quality at that—than you've had the entire year we were room-mates. Frankly, I wouldn't be surprised if it was more action than you've ever had in your entire mousey life."

Tears of anger and shame pricked my eyes. However, as defeated and humiliated as I felt, I wouldn't let her see how much she was getting under my skin. And above all, I wouldn't let her do to Vazul what she had in store for him. Even if I ended up losing him in the long run, it would never be to a hag like her.

"Thanks for your leniency," I said with as much sarcasm and contempt as I could muster. "But the answer stays no. I'm not letting you exploit him. The mere fact that you're standing here trying to convince me to hand him over to you confirms that you have no right to him. If he was yours, you wouldn't be here throwing idle threats to bully me into giving you what you want. You would have just taken him and walked out."

"I can make your life hell, you stupid cow," Angelique hissed, pointing an angry finger at me.

"You can try," I said with a frosty expression. "But I doubt the Council of Witches will appreciate you attempting to steal another witch's familiar."

"You're not a witch, you fool. You have no coven, no protection. Who do you think the Council will side with? Me, a powerful and highly respected witch in our circle? Or you, the weak, unaffiliated little nobody who couldn't even be bothered to complete her basic training?"

This time, I truly felt defeated.

CHAPTER 7
VAZUL

A s I listened to their conversation, my blood increasingly boiled with anger. The rage I felt towards Angie would soon reach its breaking point. Coral's lack of confidence was also pissing me off. In how many different ways did I need to tell her that I was hers? And yet, listening to this drivel actually helped me identify the sore points for my Mistress.

The foolish woman seriously believed that my being a sex demon meant that I was constantly craving the most disturbed forms of debauchery possible. It didn't. It only meant that I was open to everything and anything and could provide incommensurable pleasure to my partner. I didn't have to personally enjoy whatever kink I was required to partake in. In the end, all that mattered to me was to make sure my partner had what they needed so that I could feed.

But I had my preferences and my own kinks. Even though she struggled to accept it for now, I would spend this lifetime proving to her that she more than sated my needs. Her kinks were mine, not out of duty, but because I genuinely liked all that she was into. Sex with her wasn't a chore, it was mutual pleasure for the sake of enjoyment. Feeding on her delectable emotions was just the added bonus.

Still, I loved seeing my woman's spine steadily grow as the conversation progressed. Her deep outrage over Angie implying that she would pimp me out did the funniest thing to me. It wasn't jealousy that prompted Coral's anger, but a sincere need to protect me from what she perceived as extreme exploitation and degradation. It messed with my head to once more have this confirmation that she deeply cared for me as a person and not merely property.

Previous masters had shared Angie's perspective as to what I was and how I should be used. Others at that party would have also shamelessly taken a similar approach had I belonged to them instead. But not my beautiful Coral.

Angelique's despicable voice tore me out of my musings.

"You're not a witch, you fool. You have no coven, no protection. Who do you think the Council will side with? Me, a powerful and highly respected witch in our circle? Or you, the weak, unaffiliated little nobody who couldn't even be bothered to complete her basic training?"

Fed up, I stomped out of the room and marched to the entrance.

"She does have protection. Me," I growled, slamming my fist on my chest. "I told you to stay the fuck away from my Coral and to stop threatening or distressing her."

Coral gaped at me, seeming both relieved and unsure how to handle the situation. So I took charge. Walking up to the two women, I gently moved my Mistress to the side so that the wretched hag would have no choice but to face me instead.

Despite the sliver of fear that surged within her, Angelique took on a defiant stance that might have commanded respect under different circumstances.

"Pfft! She's so weak that she's ordered her servant to defend her?" Angelique asked, her voice dripping with disdain.

"My Coral did no such thing," I replied with as much contempt as I could muster. "I protect her because I *want* to. I'm not yours, never was, and never will be. For months, you tried to hatch me and miserably failed. Ever wondered why?"

"Apparently, because you were defective," she said, trying to hide the uncertainty taking root within.

"No, you stupid wench. I didn't hatch because I refused to spawn for *you*. Everything about you is foul. I *chose* not to hatch because I would never serve such an entitled and self-serving hag. You do not deserve all the ways in which one such as I could enrich your life. But the minute I felt Coral, I knew she was the one."

The shock and outrage that swelled within Angelique was literally orgasmic. Who would have thought that anything about that disgusting woman could get me excited? Obviously, not in terms of getting frisky with her in any way. But I couldn't deny the pleasure making her miserable provided me. And that was even more delightfully compounded by Coral feeling deeply moved by my words.

"Two hours was all that Coral needed for me to rise from the depths of the netherworld and rush to her. She is the Mistress I've always dreamt of serving. Her emotions are like the purest ambrosia. Her touch is an addictive drug I never want to be cured of. I crave everything about her, her presence, her voice, even her contemplative silence is a delight to me. But everything about you is repulsive. Every time you laid your filthy paws on me at your event made my skin crawl."

"You lie!" Angelique shouted, her hands fisted as she fought tears of humiliation.

"I do not lie. And knowing that my words are the truth infuriates you right now," I said with malicious glee. "You can stop spewing all that nonsense. Coral doesn't have to ask me to do chores for her. I ache to perform them because I love how pleasing her feels. Should she ever cast me away, I will return to the underworld before I ever serve the likes of you."

I took a few more steps forward, towering over the insufferable hag. She took a couple of steps back, angry, intimidated, and still unable to accept that things hadn't gone her way.

"As my woman said, you relinquished ownership of the egg when you left it in your apartment. The egg is no more. It is hatched and incinerated. You have no claim here. Now leave and do not return. Should you ever threaten or harass my Mistress again, you will feel my wrath. And remember well, I am not bound by mortal laws," I growled menacingly.

"The Council of Witches will hear of this!" Angelique snapped, her eyes throwing daggers as she glanced in turn at my woman and me.

"By all means, go cry to them and see what response you will get for trying to steal a familiar," I replied mockingly.

With an enraged growl, Angelique turned around and stormed out of the house. I casually strolled to the door, properly closing it behind her and locking it before facing my woman.

The awe and powerful emotion with which Coral gazed upon me turned me upside down.

"What incredibly kind things to say about me," she said with a slightly trembling voice.

I huffed. "It wasn't kind, it was true."

She blinked and gaped at me with an uncertain look in her beautiful light-brown eyes.

"Really? You can choose who to hatch for?" Coral asked hesitantly.

"Yes, you silly female. I told you I don't lie. I hatched for *you* because I wanted to belong to *you*."

Her lips quivered, and the wave of emotions she blasted my way nearly had me come undone. Never in my thousand years of existence had anyone ever expressed this kind of feeling for me.

Coral ran and threw herself into my arms. I caught her, and

she wrapped her arms around my neck and legs around my waist before crushing my lips with a brutal kiss. Too soon, she ended it to look at me with adoration.

"You truly are the best," she said, her voice thick with emotion.

"I know," I said smugly while smirking at her. "Feel free to thank me properly for it."

She burst out laughing then sank her fingers into my hair before rubbing her nose against mine.

"I think you deserve it," she whispered against my lips.

She didn't have to say it twice.

I carried her up to the master bedroom, our mouths locked in a passionate kiss. Her steadily growing arousal was the most potent aphrodisiac. As a sex demon, I could get hard on demand. But with her, I didn't even have to will my cock into action. Her mere presence, her slightest emotions sufficed to send blood rushing to my groin. Even now, I ached to bury myself to the hilt and pound her sweet, sweet pussy into oblivion as she writhed beneath me and screamed my name.

And soon, she would do just that, over and over again.

My cock throbbed in anticipation as I reached the landing and made a beeline for the bedroom. I kicked the door open with a bit more force than necessary, but my blood was boiling with impatience. You'd think I was a teenager about to get his dick wet for the first time instead of an elder demon with over a thousand years of existence.

I set her back down on her feet near the bed, my lips still devouring hers. My hands feverishly roamed over her as she reciprocated. I unzipped the back of her dress, my palm slipping under the fabric to caress the soft skin of her back. She shivered against me, the warmth of my palm causing goosebumps to erupt all over her. I loved how responsive she was to my touch, and especially how sensitive she was to my play on heat variations.

My beautiful Mistress had no idea what I had in store for her today.

I gently raked my claws in an ascending path up her back before hooking them under the straps of her maxi dress. I slipped them down her shoulders, and the fabric fell off in a soft rustle, exposing the perfection of her naked body to my greedy hands.

As if she had read my intentions, Coral broke the kiss first. But before I could tilt her head back to kiss her neck, my woman pre-emptively performed it on me first. I wanted to growl in protest. I liked being in charge in the bedroom. However, her emotions shouted loudly her desire to take the lead right now. The selfish part of me wanted to ignore it, but my need to please her took precedence, and I begrudgingly submitted.

How odd that I would struggle with allowing someone to voluntarily cater to me instead of having to request or even beg for it.

Coral kissed and licked my neck, her blunt fingernails scratching my back just the way I liked. It wasn't hard enough to break skin, but with enough conviction to give a nice burn. She rose to her tip toes to nip at my pointy ears. After so many centuries of existence, it had been a shock for me to discover that I loved getting my ears a little roughed up, especially getting the tip nibbled.

Our first few times together, she'd been so hesitant and insecure in her ability to please me. Silly female. She didn't understand how addicted I was to everything that was her. But seeing her steadily grow more confident, bold, and assertive was the biggest turn on. Coral was shedding her inhibitions, casting out the doubts that held her back, and finally coming into her own. I loved seeing her embrace the formidable woman that had always lurked beneath the surface, just waiting to emerge in all her glory.

She bit my earlobe hard, keeping it just this side of painful. The voluptuous moan it wrested from me had her chuckling with a smugness that had my cock grow even harder. Coral brushed her lips down my neck, sucking on the palpitating vein there before pursuing her journey south. She lingered on my nipples, tweaking them with a fierce pinch before soothing the sting with her tongue. It swirled around the areola in a lascivious way that fanned the lava bubbling in the pit of my stomach.

Where she would have slowly made her way down to my nether region with some hesitancy in the past, my woman no longer had any such qualms. Then again, she found out that whenever she tried to take control, she had to get down to business quickly before my burning need to take over eventually got the best of me. Even now, I knew I wouldn't last very long. My mouth was watering at the prospect of devouring her. It was a hunger that even ten lifetimes wouldn't suffice for me to sate.

My stomach quivered when she crouched before me, her tongue leaving a blazing trail down my abdominal muscles, past my navel, and then straight to my groin. I took a hissy breath when Coral wrapped her hand around the base of my cock. She gave it a couple of strokes, then licked her lips with a hungry look that nearly had me coming undone right there and then.

According to her, I tasted like a peach cobbler. And by the emotions emanating from her every time she put her mouth on me, she truly enjoyed it. Worse still, the wretched female showed up a couple of times in the workshop with a serving of peach cobbler and made a show of eating it in the most suggestive fashion, taking her sweet time to lick her spoon in a way that left little to the imagination. Naturally, she would do that when I was in the midst of performing a task that couldn't be paused without ruining the piece I was working on.

Needless to say I made her answer for it later.

A feral growl vibrated through my chest when she took me in her mouth and immediately set a fast pace as she bobbed in front of me. Coral twisted her wrist just the right way with each motion, giving the base a tight squeeze in the process. But it was the way she sucked on my head, teased it with her tongue, and grazed her teeth on the ridges of my length that drove me insane with pleasure.

With the fingers of both hands sunk deep into the tight curls of her hair, I ground my teeth to keep myself from rocking in and out of her mouth. The pleasure was too intense. If I gave in, I risked hurting her. And then, she started digging her nails between the seams of my ridges with her right hand while squeezing my balls with her left. The moment she realized how much pleasure both those actions procured me, she made sure never to miss an opportunity to do it.

It blew my mind how attentive Coral always was to my responses, seeking new ways to please me instead of just taking what I had to offer. That's stupid guilt attempted to rear its head again, but I squashed it. It was the oddest conundrum that making *her* happy simply required for me to let her bring *me* joy.

But all such benevolent thoughts flew right out the window the moment she took me deep into her mouth and began to hum. The vibration would make me climax in no time, which was absolutely unacceptable. My woman would scream my name many times before I would find my own release.

Without even thinking, I summoned my fire and whipped out a fiery tentacle which I wrapped around her neck. It squeezed hard enough to make her gasp, stop, and peer up at me with a mix of shock and outrage. Obviously, I controlled the heat of the flame so that it didn't actually burn and merely acted like a rope. But I intended to play with that a bit more, shortly.

Eyes locked with her, I yanked on the fiery leash, forcing her to get back onto her feet. The bright light illuminating her face indicated that my eyes were glowing as I fed on her emotions. Before she could emit the slightest complaint, I crushed her mouth with mine, my tongue invading hers like a rampaging army. She melted against me, although her hand went straight back to my cock.

I allowed her to stroke me a few more times before I broke the kiss and emulated the attentions she previously gave me. I licked and laved her nipples, pinching and nipping at them just the way she liked. However, as much as my woman enjoyed getting her breasts fondled, having attention paid to her clit was what she truly craved. And I fully intended to deliver on that front.

I kissed my way down to her stomach, teased her outie navel, and then knelt before her to stare at my prize.

"I wasn't done pleasuring you," Coral muttered with half-hearted disapproval when I leaned forward to give her engorged little nub a lick.

I glanced up at her with an unrepentant look as my fingers teased her seam, already glistening with her arousal.

"You can continue later. It's your fault for tasting so damn good. And I am hungry. I must feast," I said shamelessly.

I lifted her left leg over my shoulder and buried my face between her thighs. Coral's hands immediately latched on to my horns. I fucking loved when she did that. I licked and sucked on her clit, her delightful moans filling my ears, and her pleasure washing over me in a steady flow that I greedily gorged on.

How could anyone taste so damn good? How could mere emotions fill me even more than draining someone's lifeforce? And yet, with each intimate moment with my woman, her taste seemed to grow even more divine.

I devoured her with relentless hunger, my fingers dipping in and out of her until she started nearing the edge. I abruptly lifted her right leg to place it on my other shoulder. Coral gasped between two moans, her grip tightening around my horns in panic. She yelped when I rose to my feet, my tongue replacing my fingers inside her as I dipped it in and out in a frenzy.

She began gyrating, her legs shaking on each side of my face as her climax grew closer. I extended a fiery tendril again, and this time used it to whip that scrumptious behind of hers. It was hard enough for her to feel a pleasant sting, but nothing that would mark her flawless skin or actually inflict any type of pain.

Coral loved many aspects of BDSM, but she definitely wasn't into pain or humiliation. She liked experiencing it on the lighter side. The trust with which she abandoned herself to my care did the most wondrous thing to me. It also made me feel even more protective of her. I wanted my mistress to fulfill every single one of her fantasies while feeling safe and respected.

By the emotions radiating from her and the voluptuous sounds tumbling out of her throat, my woman more than agreed with my ministrations. And too soon, she cried out, swept away by bliss. I continued to feast on her for a while longer, until she began to return to reality. Then, I pulled my tongue out of her and abruptly tossed her onto the bed.

Her startled scream as she flew through the air before landing on the soft cushion of the mattress resonated straight in my cock. It poked at the hunter that lurked deep within me. My female craved a bit of danger, which fed my own predatory tendencies. I whipped two fiery tentacles at her, grabbing her by the ankles, and yanking her towards the edge of the bed. She yelped again with a mixture of fright and excitement.

I deliberately took on my more demonic appearance, the frightening one I used when going into combat. Lethal spikes protruded from parts of my body, my mouth widened, my teeth extended into vicious daggers, while each of my horns split into two spears also covered in spikes. My eyes glowed with a terrifying red haze that would have any sane mortal run for their lives.

A shiver coursed through my woman. The sight of her essence trickling out of her sex exposed to my hungry eyes whipped my blood into a frenzy. As terrifying as she found my battle appearance, it turned her on so much that she was visibly getting wetter at the thought of what I would do to her.

She was fucking perfect.

"Touch yourself," I ordered, my voice sounding doubled and otherworldly.

Another violent shiver coursed through her even as she complied. Although I had just spent a good while feasting on her, my mouth watered, and my cock throbbed watching her dainty fingers slip between her thighs. Watching her painted nails rubbing her clit had me on the verge of throwing myself on her before unleashing my passion.

I growled again and wrapped my hand around my cock, stroking myself almost brutally as she pleasured herself for me. She licked her lips in a slow and provocative fashion while fondling her breast with her spare hand.

My fiery tentacles tightened around her ankles, and I summoned a third one which slithered the length of her legs in a searing caress before probing her opening. Coral's breath hitched as I started inserting it inside of her.

"Do not stop," I snapped menacingly when the motion of her fingers rubbing her clit faltered.

Her body jerked in surprise. Eyes wide, she complied, the movement of her fingers accelerating in tandem with my tentacle thrusting in and out of her. The bolts of pleasure shooting out of her slammed into me in a steady flow as she once more began to crest. The shadowy tentacle inside her swelled and ebbed, maximizing the sensation it procured with each stroke, and rubbing against her G-spot just the way it needed to.

Eyes closed, her breathing labored, my woman prepared to topple over. She was so damn beautiful, her lips parted, her skin flushed with pleasure, and her gorgeous face dissolved in an air of pure bliss. And then it struck her.

Coral threw her head back with a sharp cry as a second orgasm claimed her. Her hand tightened in an almost brutal grip over her sex while the other one fisted the blanket. Her body seized for a few seconds before relaxing. However, her head rolled from side to side on the mattress as she rode the waves of ecstasy, my tentacle making love to her prolonging her rapture a little longer.

As she slowly began to refocus on me, I pulled the tentacle out of her and started wrapping it all around her.

"What... what are you doing?!" Coral stammered when I tightly bound her.

"Binding you, my sweet, before I have my way with you."

Fear and excitement surged within her in equal measure as the fiery ropes crawled all over her, forming an intricate web around her body like a rope harness. Humans called this type of bondage the art of Shibari and Kinbaku.

My ropes didn't bind her wrists behind her back. Instead, two of them tugged on her arms, forcing her first into a sitting position and then to lean forward.

Coral gasped when the tentacles bound her right wrist and ankle together, and the right elbow and knee together. With the same thing happening with her left leg and arm, my Mistress found herself trapped in a crab tie.

Two fiery pillars appeared to shoot out from the floor—with an impressive flash of light, for theatrics—that had my woman shouting in fear again. A blazing rope whipped out from the top of each pillar, wrapping around her bound hands and ankles before yanking her up. The emotions blasting out of my woman as she found herself in horizontal suspension, face up, had me so fucking hard I nearly spilled.

"Do you know how beautiful you are? Bound, exposed, and helpless but to take all that I'm about to unleash on you?" I said in that threatening otherworldly voice.

She started breathing in short, shallow bursts. Heart pounding, her pupils dilated, and her lips parted, Coral watched me approach with fearful anticipation. More of her essence glistened on her slit as I reached for her thighs with both hands. Her breath hitched when my long, monstrous claws slightly dug into her tender flesh, although without breaking skin.

"I'm going to wreck you," I hissed in half a whisper, summoning an inferno to rage around the room.

Still in my battle form, I pushed my cock into her opening. In a perfect world, I would have rammed myself home with unbridled savagery, but that would have harmed her. Still, I didn't insert myself in as careful and gentle a way as I normally did. Closely monitoring her emotions allowed me to gauge what level of discomfort matched her fantasy of being ravaged by a demon.

In no time, I was fully sheathed. The way her inner walls sucked me in and then contracted greedily around my cock had bestial growls rising in my throat with the need to spill. I immediately set a punishing pace, taking her fast and increasingly hard until I was pounding into her with reckless abandon. Each stroke, each caress of her tight sheath around my length had liquid flames coursing through my veins.

While I actually kept the visual inferno surrounding us at room temperature, the one raging inside me had me on the verge of combusting. Coral was shouting with pleasure, making unintelligible sounds as I destroyed her. Watching my cock sinking in and out of her as she hung helplessly, bound to my fire pillars, was the most erotic thing I had ever experienced.

My woman wouldn't last much longer. Neither would I for that matter. I gradually raised the heat level of my fiery tendrils woven in an intricate network around her body. I raked my claws over her skin so they, too, would inflict a nice burn, even as my cock also flared inside her. My Coral would sustain no harm, but she was truly experiencing the safe simulation of being desecrated by a fiery demon in the deepest pits of hell.

Her climax slammed into her with earth-shattering violence. My knees nearly buckled under the powerful wave of pleasure nearly too much to bear that crashed into me. My woman's inner walls clamping down on my cock did me in.

I roared and threw my head back as a devastating orgasm claimed me. On instinct, I buried myself deep inside Coral in one brutal thrust. Liquid bliss shot out of me like an erupting volcano as I filled my Mistress to the brim. Each spurt felt like literal pieces of my soul being torn out of me and offered as sacrifice to the woman who owned me like no one ever had or ever would.

Feeling faint, I snuffed out the inferno raging around us. In my half-dazed state, I might lose control of the temperature and actually burn the entire place down. My fiery ropes also faded, releasing my Coral from her bondage. I carefully gathered her in my arms as her bindings unwound and lowered her to the mattress.

She snuggled against me, her body still shaking from the lingering throes of passion, as was mine. I tightened my embrace as an almost rabid possessiveness surged within me. For centuries, I wandered the depths of the underworld only to occasionally walk the Mortal Plane for the short lifespan of the human masters I hadn't despised, but who I had also not felt particular affection for.

But Coral was my one and only. My search was finally at an end. I was home.

"I'm never letting you go," I whispered.

My Mistress didn't answer. But she didn't need to. She snuggled deeper into me and a rainbow of joy blasted out of her, responding to my statement in the most powerful way possible.

I smiled.

CHAPTER 8
VAZUL

The morning prior to the fair, I switched back to my human form in order to escort Coral to the Council of Witches' headquarters. Today, she would get my official papers so that I could finally be the one driving her around as well as running errands with my own bank account and card. We would also be able to travel together anywhere without me having to fly separately in my fire wisp form as I wouldn't otherwise be able to show proper ID.

It still bothered me that Coral insisted that I would be a formal employee with a regular salary instead of her servant. She actually suggested at first that I should be her partner, but I shut that down. Although she relented, her emotions broadcast loudly that she would bring it back up later once we were more established in our routine. I was curious to see who would give in first.

That said, she could have ordered me to simply comply. But once more, she chose to respect my wishes and not impose her will. It was odd to be treated like a person instead of property. And I fucking loved it.

A wave of possessiveness swelled within me as I glanced at

my Mistress. I never imagined tender emotions would ever have their place in my life. And yet, there it was.

Once my paperwork was sorted out, we would head out to the venue so that Coral could get registration out of the way, get our badges, and scope out our setup location. It was silly how excited I felt about it. I wanted my woman to shine. And I didn't doubt for a minute that she would, especially now that she actually got the spells sorted out for the haunted alley insert of the coffee table showstopper.

However, shortly after the car took off, a sense of unease washed over me. It took me a moment to realize that it was a wave of malicious and triumphant emotions that had crawled their way to me. I straightened in my seat and opened my senses wide to scan the people nearby.

"Something's wrong," I said, my back stiff.

"What?" Coral asked, her voice filled with worry as she glanced at me before having to look back at the road as she had been about to make a left turn. "What's going on?"

"I must go back to the house," I said, my voice tense.

"Okay, let me make a U-turn at the next—"

"No," I said sternly, taking her aback. "Keep going. Just drop me off at the next intersection. I recognize the source of the threat. She must continue to think that the house is empty."

"She? Is it Angie?" Coral asked, anger seeping into her voice.

I didn't have to speak for her to understand. The look on my face was all the confirmation she needed. Her anger swelled.

"I'm going to kick that bitch's ass so hard!" Coral snapped.

I chuckled. "You're sexy when you're angry. But there will be time later for you to punish her. Fear not, my Coral. All will be well. Do not approach the house before I give you the go ahead."

Although clearly unhappy about it, my woman complied. I indicated the spot where she was to leave me, right next to a narrow cul-de-sac alley between two large buildings. As soon as she dropped me off, I hurried to the darkest shadow before turning into my wisp form. It pissed me off that I had to leave my clothes behind as I had dressed rather fashionably to make my Mistress proud. Hopefully, they would still be here for me to recover once I was done dealing with the wretched female.

As it was broad daylight, zipping through the sky in my fiery form would attract too many eyes. The modern-day world had become quite a pain with all the surveillance technology available. It was almost impossible nowadays to go anywhere without some form of camera tracking you. Instead, I turned into a blue flame as it would more easily be mistaken for a drone or some form of metallic flying object.

I soared high in the sky to make myself even harder to detect as I raced back to the house. Even as I began my descent, I spotted Angelique's vehicle. She was pulling up a short distance from our home. I dashed towards the house and flew down the chimney while she was too distracted parking her vehicle to see me enter.

As I suspected she was coming here to destroy Coral's collection, I immediately set up the camera my Mistress usually used to record her social media videos. Hopefully, it wouldn't be required. But irrefutable evidence of her vandalism attempt would give Coral all the ammunition necessary to crush the wretched woman.

Personally, I wanted to dispose of her with far more fiendish methods, but I doubted my woman would approve. Furthermore, if Angelique was seen entering the house before she went missing, it would put Coral in a difficult position. I wouldn't be the reason for her downfall.

I positioned the camera in a way to cover as much of the room as possible and placed a miniature bush next to it so that it would hide the light indicating that it was active. With all the other objects on that shelf, it would be nearly impossible for

Angelique to even notice it unless she knew specifically what to look for.

When the seconds turned to minutes, I carefully approached the entrance to peer outside. Angie was still sitting inside her car, biding her time before she made her move, likely to make certain we wouldn't return to grab something we might have forgotten.

To my dismay, she finally got out of the car. Except, it wasn't Angelique, but Coral who stepped out. A burning anger surged within me that the foul female should dare take on my woman's appearance. It was a very good glamour spell. Anyone who walked past her would be fooled. She even perfectly emulated the elegant way in which Coral's hips swayed when she walked.

I hastened back to the workshop and settled in the hearth as a slow burning fire.

The possibility that she was coming here to set some sort of curse instead or plant something incriminating to harm Coral crossed my mind. But I immediately dismissed it. Angie would know that I would detect any curse as soon as I entered the room where it was cast.

Moments later, the sound of the front door opening reached me. I summoned every ounce of my willpower to keep myself calm. If I became angry, my flames would flare and potentially give away my presence. While she would likely question the fire in the hearth, she saw me leaving with Coral and therefore had no reason to suspect I had returned. But even if she figured it out, her mere illegal presence here was enough to get her in trouble.

The way her footsteps came directly to the workshop indicated that she had been here before. It further infuriated me that she would abuse the hospitality my woman previously showed her in order to cause harm. My heart leapt when the door opened. The flabbergasted expression on Angie's face would have been delightfully priceless if I wasn't so focused on reining myself in.

A series of extremely unladylike swear words tumbled out of

her mouth as she took in every element of the collection. But it was the coffee table showstopper that truly triggered her. She gaped in disbelief at the ghostly animations appearing in various locations along the miniature Victorian street. The flickering lamppost and randomized illuminated windows were also in full effect.

"All of this should be mine, you thief," Angelique said angrily through her teeth. "You're going to regret fucking with me. No one takes from me and gets away with it."

A wave of hatred shot out of Angelique, followed by a powerful urge to destroy. It slammed into me with nearly debilitating strength. I almost surged forward to intervene, but I once more reined myself in. For all her faults, Angie was far too devious to just smash things in a fit of rage. That would leave undeniable proof of vandalism.

As much as she wanted to destroy my woman, she didn't want it to be traceable back to her. It needed to look like an accident. She glanced around the room, looking for something she could use to cause irreparable damage in a way that would be attributed to bad luck or the unfortunate outcome of neglect or distraction.

Her gaze suddenly landed on the fireplace. It was eerie having her stare directly at me without even realizing that it wasn't a bunch of dancing flames filling the hearth, but the very demon she coveted.

"Stupid, stupid girl," Angelique whispered with a devilish grin. "You should know better than to leave a fire burning when no one is in the house. What a pity if a devastating accident were to occur."

The malicious way she cackled made even me uneasy. She looked at various objects around the room, trying to strategize as to which would be best suited for what she had in mind. She finally settled on a big roll of wrapping paper. She brought it next to the fireplace and started looking for the right angle to lean the roll against it.

It confused me at first, and then understanding dawned on me. The extra packing boxes she added, positioning them in a way that almost created a continuous path between the fireplace and the coffee table clarified everything. Their placement wouldn't even be deemed intentional during a forensic evaluation. It could easily pass for poor judgment or lack of awareness in favor of convenience.

The calculated and evil way in which she plotted the whole thing would have been impressive had the target not been someone I cared so deeply for. The worst part was that this hatred didn't even make sense. Coral and Angie didn't have a long history of rivalry. Technically, she was no threat to her. But people like Angelique couldn't stand the thought of someone else existing or thriving in their space. They needed to crush and dominate in order to soothe their fragile egos and deep-rooted insecurities.

Once her dirty work was completed, she toppled the big roll of wrapping paper so parts of it would touch the fire in the hearth. Too bad for her, that fire was me. I fought the urge to laugh out loud. Even in this form, I could address people. It wasn't like telepathy. They would actually hear me through their ears. For a split second, I considered messing with her head by doing so. But I wanted to get a bit more footage recorded before I revealed myself.

Playing along, I slithered over the wrapping paper, quickly spreading myself around the boxes and other flammable objects nearby. As I could control the heat I emitted—like during my naughty time with my woman—I didn't burn most of the items I touched. However, without smoke or darkening paper, Angie would realize that something was amiss. So I did scorch a few expendable things like the surface layers of the wrapping paper and one of the boxes.

She gasped, seeing how quickly the fire spread. Obviously, it was a tactic on my part so that she wouldn't see that I wasn't truly destroying anything of value. I projected the heat towards her, while keeping a cool bubble underneath to protect the collection.

She cackled gleefully. "I told you not to mess with me, you pathetic little cunt. You should have taken my offer while you could. I'll drink your tears in a champagne flute while I ride *my* Liderc's cock."

This time, I couldn't hold back my anger, which translated into a giant fiery flare. She gasped again, realizing that sticking around any longer wouldn't be wise. Turning on her heel, she hurried towards the door to exit the workshop. Not wanting to let her escape so easily, I spread my flames into a fiery fist with which I slammed the door shut. Angelique yelped and stumbled a few steps back. Shock quickly gave way to fear as her mind processed what just happened.

As I shifted back into my demon form, I directed the flames to surround the foul woman with a fiery ring. She spun around and went pale when our eyes met. I didn't need a mirror to see how terrifying I likely looked right this instant. When going into battle, each of my horns split into two, and vicious spikes covered them. More deadly spikes spread over my arms in parts of my body. My mouth widened and filled with countless night-marish teeth that could pierce through metal and bones. But unlike during the sexy scenario with my woman, this time, far more spikes covered my body, and my face was even more nightmarish.

"What did I tell you, you stupid wench?" I growled in a menacing tone.

"You... you can't be here!" Angelique stuttered, shaking her head in denial while taking a step back. "You left! I saw you leave with her!"

"And I came back when I felt your stench nearby," I snarled

while slowly advancing towards her. "Did I not warn you what would happen if you crossed my Mistress again?"

"I'm sorry! It was foolish of me. I was just hurt. I spent so many months and effort just trying to get your egg and then even more months trying to hatch you. Don't you see how much I wanted you. Seeing you finally here and belonging to another made me lose my mind. I just wanted to have you. I'm sorry," she said pleadingly while retreating as far as the flames behind her allowed.

"I don't give a fuck what you wanted. I told you what would happen if you tried anything ever again. Now, it is time for you to reap what you sowed."

"NO!" she shouted, her voice shaking with fear. "Other than to feed, you are forbidden to harm humans!"

I waved a dismissive hand. "I am allowed to protect my Mistress from those who would harm her. You deliberately threatened her livelihood. Not only did you trespass in her home, her safe haven with evil intent, but you also dared to defile her likeness with your glamour. REMOVE IT, you foul wench!" I shouted.

"I'm sorry!" Angie exclaimed, fumbling to cast the incantation to dispel the glamour. "Please, let me go. I promise never to cause harm again. I will take a blood oath to never interfere in your lives anymore."

"Oh, you definitely won't. I'm making sure of it. Permanently."

"No! Mercy!"

True terror descended over her features when she saw the fiery streaks ignite beneath my skin, and my hands turned an angry shade of red as power built up, ready to be unleashed. By entering the house wearing Coral's appearance, Angelique forfeited the one thing that could have protected her from my wrath. No one, no recording would show her entering this place.

Once she went missing, there would be no tying her to my Mistress.

The foolish woman attempted to cast a protection spell—not that it could have done anything against me. She shrieked when blisters immediately formed over her hands and mouth as I countered her.

An evil chuckle tumbled out of my throat.

"Do you know what they do to evil witches, little Angelique?" I asked in a sickly-sweet voice. "They burn them at the stake. But in your case, maybe I should just drain you and use that extra energy to further elevate my Mistress. That would be poetic justice, don't you think?"

Crying, Angelique begged and pleaded in an endless sputtering string of barely intelligible words through her blistered lips and tongue.

Although draining her would have indeed given me extra power to use to the benefit of my Coral, I wanted no part of Angie inside me in any shape or form.

"No one will miss you," I said as two bolts of fire began to swirl above my open palms.

Just as I was about to unleash them on the wretched female, the workshop door burst open, startling us both.

"Liderc, stop!"

Stunned, I gaped at the elegant, older woman standing beyond the flames by the door.

How the fuck did I not feel her approach?

"Mrs. Hopkins!" Angie exclaimed, shock and hope filling her voice.

CHAPTER 9
CORAL

S itting in my car, utterly traumatized, I watched Vazul run into the alley, moments before a blue flame shot towards the sky. It flew by so fast, had I not been looking in that direction, I definitely would have missed it. You couldn't even clearly see him as he flew towards the house. At best, it resembled a blur.

Although he told me to keep going, I didn't want to drive away. A big fat pile of stinking poo was about to hit the fan. And I wanted to be there to keep things from escalating to the point of no return.

On instinct, I hopped out of the car and went to fetch the clothes he had discarded. I got back into my vehicle and drove to the nearest grocery store so that I could park without drawing too much attention. Just as I was entering the lot, my phone beeped with an incoming notification. Curious, I hurried to a free spot, put the car on park, then whipped out my phone.

My heart skipped a beat when I realized it was my front door camera alerting me to a person walking up to the door. I immediately turned on the camera feed on my phone. Seeing myself entering my own home freaked me out beyond words. Obviously, I understood that this was someone—most probably Angelique—using a glamour spell to emulate my likeness. But would she be so bold as to do the dirty work herself? Could she have conned, sweet talked, or coerced one of her sycophants to do the deed in her stead?

My instinctive reaction was to dial 911. But before I even finished typing the three digits, I paused and reconsidered. There would be too much explanation to give between Vazul in the house without papers, Angelique possibly still under the glamour spell to mimic me, and the footage on the security camera.

The moment we were introduced to the craft, we were told in no uncertain terms that there would be hell to pay if we ever exposed the secret world we evolved in. I hung up without completing the call and dialed the emergency number of the Council of Witches instead. To my relief, the receptionist—a man with a truly amazing voice—responded before the first ring was even done.

"You have reached the Council. How may I help you?"

"Someone using glamour has broken into my house. I fear things might get ugly between that intruder and my familiar," I replied.

"Is this number your personal line?" the man asked.

"Yes."

"Very well, Coral. Are you currently at home?"

It always disturbed me how much information society now possessed about me and everyone else with something as simple as your phone number. But now was not the time to dwell on this.

"No. I'm in the parking lot of a grocery store nearby," I replied before giving him a quick breakdown of the situation.

"Go home and calm your familiar," he ordered. "Someone will be there shortly to handle the matter. Something like this was expected."

I opened my mouth to ask him what he meant by that, but he

had already hung up. For a split second, I considered calling him back but thought better of it. I raced back to the house, cussing at the wretched traffic that seemed to have suddenly come out of nowhere. For half a beat, I contemplated just leaving the car by the sidewalk and running the rest of the way home. Obviously, that was a dumb idea, but being stuck behind a bunch of cars moving slowly made me feel helpless while my fertile imagination went into overdrive.

I knew too little about the rules regarding summoners and their minions. A familiar had the right to cause harm to protect their master. But to what degree? How far would Vazul go? What would be deemed excessive force? What would *I* be okay with him doing based on the current circumstances?

The answer to that popped into my head with a certainty that left me reeling. As much as I wanted Angelique to get her proper comeuppance, I didn't want her to face any physical harm, least of all of a lethal nature.

I finally pulled up to my street only to see two familiar women walking up to my door. Had I not been sitting in my car, I would have fallen on my ass upon seeing Mrs. Hopkins in the lead followed by Myrtle—the Head Priestess of Angie's coven.

How the hell did they get here so fast?

Above all, what the fuck was Mrs. Hopkins doing here? Seeing her open my front door with a flick of her hand broke my mind even more. How had I not known that she also was a witch? The ease with which she opened the door broadcast loudly that she had to be extremely powerful. That she would be the one sent to handle this situation also indicated that she ranked very high within the organization.

I parked in my driveway and ran into the house. My heart sank at the sight of the red and orange flickering glow typical of the light emitted by a fire. Tears pricked my eyes at the burnt smell, even as my brain wondered at the absence of thick, dark smoke.

"Mrs. Hopkins!" I heard Angie call from within my workshop, her voice filled with a mix of fear and relief, although she spoke in a strangely muddled fashion.

I ran down the hallway and all but shoved Myrtle out of the way to assess the extent of the damage done to what should have been the beginning of my dream career and foundation of my business. So many years of hard work and sacrifice all gone up in flames because of the entitled jealousy of a vicious, self-centered, spoiled brat.

My brain froze when I saw Vazul looking terrifying, standing a short distance from Angelique, a ring of fire raging around her keeping her caged. And all around them, my entire collection stood unscathed. The only signs of visible damage appeared to be on a portion of my roll of wrapping paper, and a charred, empty box.

I nearly wept with relief as I stood there, too stunned to speak or otherwise react. Seeing me, Vazul immediately doused the fire burning inside him. The balls of flames swirling over his open palms fizzled out, the glowing streaks under his skin faded. His face lost its evil demonic appearance and returned to the handsome male I was falling for, his horns merging back into a single pair as the vicious spikes on his body receded into his skin.

This monstrous appearance should have frightened me, but it didn't. I was only relieved that he never got to unleash the wrath Angelique brought upon herself. To my even bigger relief, Vazul dissipated the ring of fire restraining my nemesis.

She immediately attempted to run towards the exit of the workshop, but with a single gesture of her hand, Mrs. Hopkins froze Angie in place. Frozen actually wasn't quite the appropriate description. It was more as if she hit an invisible wall, stumbled back, then had her feet locked into place. She still seemed to have control of the rest of her body.

The gaping fish expression that settled on her face undoubtedly matched mine—although my stupid mind kept picturing a shocked Pikachu. Myrtil stood there quietly, looking both angry and defeated.

What the fuck is going on?!

"I am the High Witch Examiner of the Council," Mrs. Hopkins said with a voice cold enough to send us right back to the Ice Age. "Serious accusations have been levied against you, Angelique Delaney. And your presence here appears to confirm their accuracy."

High Witch Examiner of the Council?!

Under different circumstances, I'd be falling on my ass again in shock. How had she fooled us this entire time? How did Angie and Sophia not know who we were actually dealing with? But Angie running her mouth again wiped all those wandering thoughts right out of my mind.

"He tried to kill me to silence me!" Angelique exclaimed, pointing an accusatory finger at Vazul while displaying a trauma-tized and fearful expression worthy of an Oscar.

"What? To silence you about what? You broke into my house!" I exclaimed, outraged.

"And then tried to set my mistresses miniature collection on fire out of jealousy and spite," Vazul said, his voice thick with anger and contempt.

He extended a hand towards me, and I went to him without hesitation. He drew me possessively against his side, and I instantly melted, feeling safe and protected, despite the messed-up situation we were in.

"That's a lie!" Angelique shouted. "Coral *invited* me and set me up. I should have known there was something fishy going on. We had an argument yesterday after I confronted her about stealing my Liderc. She knew I wasn't going to just take such a crime lying down. I warned her that I would bring up her theft to the Council. So she went on the offensive to stop me with this fiendish trap!"

I stared at her, flabbergasted by her sheer audacity. The most shocking part was the ease with which she spewed those lies. She did it so effortlessly and so convincingly that I would have fallen for it had I not been on the receiving end of such slander.

"That's completely false!" I exclaimed, finding my voice at last. "I did no such thing. In fact, Vazul warned her to stay away from us. She did come here yesterday demanding that I hand him over to her. But she has no grounds to reclaim what was never hers. Not only did Angelique discarded his egg, but he never hatched for her."

"You stole it before I could!" Angelique interrupted in a self-righteous tone. "If not—"

"SILENCE!" Mrs. Hopkins shouted.

Her voice resounded like thunderclap. I felt myself shrinking. Even my demon appeared impressed, not to say intimidated. The contemptuous look she gave Angelique had her withering in her shoes. As much as I despise her, I couldn't help but almost feel sorry—not to say worried—for her. That look could incinerate anyone right where they stood.

"Coral stole nothing," Mrs. Hopkins said in a frosty tone. "It was *I* who gave her the egg that you abandoned. I warned you multiple times to come fetch what you had left behind. You *chose* to forsake your belongings, knowing that if they weren't retrieved by that date, they would be disposed of. And still, you failed to do anything about it, until she came to do it."

"She came to retrieve them for *me*!" Angelique hissed.

"She came to retrieve them to avoid paying the cleaning penalty," Mrs. Hopkins countered. "Your repeated failure to reclaim those items made them fair game to be taken, given, or otherwise disposed of, including that egg. What Coral did with them after you showed such disregard was entirely up to her. But even then, you still wouldn't have any claim over the Liderc. He didn't hatch for you."

"That's unfair!" Angelique shouted. "I paid for it!"

"Then you shouldn't have abandoned it. That matter is settled," Mrs. Hopkins said dismissively before glancing around the room. "Moving on, what are you doing here? What is the purpose of your presence? And why was there a fire upon our arrival?"

"She tried to burn my Mistress' collection to harm her. She set up all of these inflammable objects by the fireplace to make it look like an accident," Vazul said in a stern voice.

"That's a lie! It is an abject set up, a trap to ensure my downfall because I threatened to bring her theft before the Council! She invited me here under the false pretense of discussing the situation so that we could reach some sort of amicable agreement. Why else would I come here? My entire coven and other friends were at my house but a couple of days ago and saw what a magnificent collection I possess. This is no threat to me. *She* is no threat to me. I have no reason to want to destroy this. I just want what is rightfully mine," Angelique argued in an impassioned tone.

Once again, had I not been the target of her lies, I might have been fooled by her acting.

"If I truly invited you, why did you enter my house with a glamour spell to impersonate me?" I challenged. "If you were expected, you would have simply walked in as yourself."

"I did no such thing!"

"You most certainly did!" I countered, while whipping out my phone. "My door cam captured you when you walked up. That's why I called the Council, because I knew you were up to no good."

"And that's not the only recording of you," Vazul said with malicious glee before gesturing towards the shelf in the corner of the workshop. "I set up Coral's camera moments before you entered. Everything you have done—and said—is right here for all to see."

"You fucking rock!" I whispered, staring at my demon with awe.

"You mortals and your technology certainly make things far more interesting than back in ancient days," Vazul said in an amused tone.

I kissed his cheek and ran to my laptop to call up the camera feed. In the few seconds it took, Angelique spewed all kinds of excuses and half-baked explanations as to what actually happened. But no one was listening to her anymore.

We watched the footage in complete disbelief. No words could describe the depth of the anger that surged within me. In that instant, I almost regretted that the High Witch Examiner had intervened when she did. Only a few seconds more, and I didn't doubt Vazul would have reduced that conniving bitch into a pile of ashes. Normally, I wouldn't advocate for violence. But she deserved all of it and more.

That would have been too short and swift of punishment.

It certainly would have been. Angie deserved to live just so that she could suffer the consequences of her actions. And by the look Mrs. Hopkins was giving her, my sweet little nemesis would definitely not be getting off easy.

"It's not what it looks like," Angie stammered, her face chalky because she'd grown so pale. "It's—"

"Enough, you foolish girl," Mrs. Hopkins interrupted sternly. "The minute the Liderc hatched, I knew you would do something stupid. We felt his entrance into this world. We stood back and watched, knowing how your greed and sense of entitlement would push you to break the rules. Why do you think we were so quick to arrive?"

Angelique cast a betrayed look at her Head Priestess. Myrtil averted her eyes, countless conflicting emotions fleeting over her features. Although it had never been proven, rumor had it that they were related. That would have explained why she allowed Angie to get away with so many things that would have otherwise gotten her kicked out of the coven. However, blood ties are not, Myrtil couldn't cross the Council to protect her relative. She would have been sworn to secrecy the moment she became aware of the investigation. Had she warned Angie, the Head Priestess would be facing a shit storm of her own right now.

"Our job is to anticipate risks that will expose us," Mrs. Hopkins continued mercilessly. "Your ego and your greed threatened to do exactly that. We also have very strict rules against abusing our powers to harm other members of our community. You broke those rules. Therefore, you will stand before the Council to answer for your crimes."

"She's not a member of our community!" Angelique screeched, her voice filled with panic, anger, and outrage. "Coral doesn't even belong to a coven. She cannot claim the protection of the Council!"

"Although a novice, she's still a witch," Mrs. Hopkins countered in a tone that brooked no argument. "As the older witch *and* one of the two who introduced her to the craft, you had a duty to protect her, not undermine her. Whether she belongs to a coven or not is irrelevant. Coral knows us and is known to us. In fact, had your malicious plans not derailed her schedule, she would be at our headquarters as we speak, formalizing the paperwork for her Liderc."

She then turned to look at Myrtil and gestured for her to approach. I had never seen the High Priestess looking so humbled, so small. Even if she had followed the rules by not giving unfair protection to Angelique, I strongly believed she got chewed out about the entire situation prior to coming here. And my gut told me that she'd get another generous earful afterwards, now that their suspicions were confirmed.

"Angelique Delaney, you have proven yourself to be reckless and dangerous," Mrs. Hopkins said in a solemn tone. "Therefore, until your trial, you shall be stripped of your power."

My jaw dropped.

"What?!" Angelique exclaimed, horrified.

Ignoring her, the High Witch Examiner glanced back at Myrtil.

"Collar your witch," Mrs. Hopkins said, gesturing with her head for her to proceed.

"No! You can't do this! Do you know who I am?!" Angie shouted.

"Enough, you foolish girl," Myrtil hissed at last under her breath. "You're in enough trouble as is. Don't make things worse. You will have the trial to defend yourself."

I couldn't tell if this was proof of a blood bond between them, or Myrtil merely attempting to limit the damage. As this scandal involved the top witch in her coven, the rumors and then the outcome would negatively impact all of them. I didn't doubt Myrtil would fight tooth and nail to obtain leniency for Angie. Even though I was the slighted party, due to the nature of the crime, I wouldn't be able to unilaterally request that they drop the charges. This was now the Council's case. Their rules had been broken. And judging by Mrs. Hopkins demeanor, she would want to make an example out of Angelique.

For the second time today—something that hadn't happened in a very long time—I felt sorry for her.

Still, she tried to resist when her head priestess placed an iron collar around her neck. It wasn't fancy, but it was delicate enough to be worn comfortably with any outfit, and even to sleep with. The runic symbols that enabled its magic neutralization effect actually made it look stylish. To the layman, it would only be deemed a cool accessory.

Once done, Myrtil escorted Angie out of the workshop. For the first time in the more than one year since I knew her, I saw genuine tears welling in Angelique's eyes and trickling down her cheeks. I couldn't begin to imagine what being stripped of her power would be like for someone like Angelique whose entire sense of worth revolved around her magic and all the things that made her superior to others. This punishment alone was a devastating blow to her. Knowing that it was only the tip of the iceberg truly challenged my empathic side.

As soon as they were out of the room, Mrs. Hopkins turned back to face me. That woman was intimidating as fuck. The rational side of me—with a proper sense of self-preservation—wanted to wither before her and stay quiet until she provided further instructions. But the other, bolder side of me—that had steadily been blossoming under the supportive and nurturing presence of my demon—decided to run its mouth.

"The bags weren't too full, were they?" I asked with a dare in my voice. "You put that egg under my armpit on purpose, didn't you?"

The smugness with which she smirked was all the confirmation I needed. Although that thought had crossed my mind on multiple occasions since Vazul hatched, proof of Mrs. Hopkins's meddling still floored me. Worse still, I struggled to accept the reality of her being a powerful witch, and that I'd been too blind to see for over a year.

"You were always the better fit," Mrs. Hopkins said with a shrug. "But you need better friends. That coven is nothing but a den of snakes. You do not belong there. Sophia is decent enough, but the others are vultures. My words don't surprise you. It was so obvious that you made no effort to join them. Smart decision, except for the part where you neglected to work on the craft."

I shifted on my feet with embarrassment. How did that woman manage to so easily make me feel like a naughty kid being chastised by her professor? Vazul caressed my back in a soothing fashion although his eyes remained glued on the High Witch Examiner.

"You must work on your magic and join a coven. You cannot stay this clueless and especially not leave your house this unprotected," Mrs. Hopkins continued sternly with an unimpressed look and her nose wrinkled as she glanced around the room.

"There isn't a single ward to be seen anywhere. Had you done the basic work, that fire Angie intended for your house wouldn't have stood a chance. In fact, her glamour and locksmith spell would have had no effect."

"She has resumed learning new spells," Vazul interjected, his tone slightly defensive as he tightened a protective arm around me.

Fuck, I could kiss him right now.

"Yeah, I have," I concurred sheepishly.

The amused smile Mrs. Hopkins cast towards Vazul before she glanced back at me softened her face in a way I had never seen before.

"I'm pleased to hear it. I will expect you at my covenstead the day after the fair is over. We'll make something out of you yet," she said in an imperious tone while giving me an assessing look.

"What?!" I breathed out, flabbergasted.

"You heard me, young lady. I'll send you the coordinates shortly. Be on time, and do not disappoint me," she said sternly.

I stood there gaping, my mind reeling. You didn't get so casually invited to join a coven, least of all one where the Head Priestess—which I assumed Mrs. Hopkins was—also happened to be a very high-ranking official within the Council of Witches. You didn't hold such a position unless you were extremely powerful. That she would invite someone like me was a tremendous compliment. Normally, you begged, groveled, and spent months—sometimes even years—trying to prove yourself worthy before they would even give you the time of day.

Her face softened again, and she smiled in an almost maternal fashion that gave me an even bigger whiplash than Vazul with his abrupt switches between being savagely honest and divinely sweet.

"It took you mere hours to hatch a Liderc who refused all others for years. Angie wasn't the first owner of that egg," Mrs.

Hopkins said in a gentle voice. "And in the short time by your side, you have earned his complete and unwavering loyalty. That, more than any test or trial I could subject you to, proves your worth. Do not be late."

With that, the High Witch Examiner—and now apparently my brand-new High Priestess—turned around and exited the room.

"I told you that you were the best," Vazul said smugly.

"No, Vazul. You are."

"That, too," he concurred.

I chuckled, playfully slapped his shoulder, and lifted my face to receive his kiss.

EPILOGUE
CORAL

The three-day fair was a roaring success. The number of people lining up around my booth nearly overwhelmed me. I had expected to receive my fair share of attention, not only because of my showstoppers, but mostly because of the way Vazul elevated my vision beyond anything I ever thought possible. The flawlessness of his craftsmanship blew everyone away. Everything looked even better in the real world than it had in my imagination.

Throughout the event, Vazul chastised me for attempting to give him credit. It baffled me how much it pissed him off, but I merely wanted to give him his due. In his eyes, I was belittling my own contribution. There was a time when he would have been right. But since he entered my life—recent though it had been—Vazul truly helped me become more assertive and recognize my worth. It was specifically because I was finally embracing my more confident side that I could so easily share the fame and praises.

I didn't need to hog all the accolades because my own contribution spoke for itself. This entire collection was *my* vision, *my* creation. I personally built more than 95% of it before he swooped in. As much as Vazul had corrected and improved the less stellar elements, he hadn't redone everything. In fact, if we were to quantify it all, he had maybe retouched, tweaked, or flat out recreated barely 10% of the entire project.

But those corrections had an incredible impact. And *that* needed to be acknowledged.

In many ways, it was like having the perfect photo shoot for the cleverest marketing campaign of all times and then having a humongous typo in the giant billboard. It didn't matter how brilliant everything else was. The only thing people would see and talk about was that wretched typo.

Without my demon's magic touch, I wouldn't have received as phenomenal a response as I did. To both my delight and dismay, I sold out so fast that I spent the last day of the event with a mostly empty booth, with a catalog and photos of my work for those who had missed all the physical items. Thankfully, the buyer of my coffee table agreed to only pick it up at the end of the convention.

By itself, that piece brought me the majority of my sales. Obviously, most people wouldn't have been able to afford it. But they loved it so much that they wanted to at least be able to claim that they owned some decorative item made by the creator of the 'Haunted Street Coffee Table' or 'Crazy Cool Table' as the attendees had taken to calling it.

The most amazing part of it all was seeing Vazul constantly hyping me up to the people who visited our booth. My brain understood that, as my Liderc, he was genetically wired to do everything in his power to make me shine. But I believed at a visceral level that he wasn't just doing it out of duty, but because he truly believed everything he was saying.

In my entire life, I had never felt more supported than by him. He believed in me and saw a beauty inside me that I never thought existed but that I was definitely starting to wholeheartedly embrace.

The icing on it all were the countless custom orders the atten-dees showered me with as well as offers to work as a miniaturist on various movie project. I had hoped to get at least a handful of orders to hold me off in the first months after opening my shop. Instead, I had so many bookings that I could actually choose which ones I really wanted to do and even turn down the ones I either wasn't inspired by or that simply couldn't fit within a reasonably attainable schedule.

The movie project collaborations were the hardest to decide on. The bragging rights alone would have anyone wanting to scream a resounding yes. Quite a few of those projects sounded thrilling on top of quite lucrative. However, after further consid-eration, I decided to pass. While I didn't doubt that I could have rocked the hell out of those projects, I'd been blessed with the possibility of working on my own custom or private projects. Working on movie sets implied ungodly hours, constant flip flopping on artistic direction, and having my creativity stunted by the needs and demands of the movie. In the majority of cases, there would be no negotiation possible. Even if you disagreed with the direction given, you had no choice but to comply.

To my complete shock and confusion, I found out that Angie had pulled out of the event. That baffled me. Her collection had been quite beautiful and would have likely sold out as well. While awaiting her trial, she was still allowed to carry on with business as usual. This fair had nothing to do directly with the Council of Witches. Even though she initially tried to sabotage my own ability to attend, the Council didn't have the power to forbid her from attending a professional engagement organized by mundane folks. So why pull out? Was it shame? Was she still too angry to go out in public, and especially anywhere near me?

Her unexpected absence fueled countless speculations, espe-cially in light of the ridiculously lame excuse she offered. The foolish woman claimed that her pet, having reached a very old age, was dying. She needed to be by its side in its final hours.

People with pets would undoubtedly have sided with her. But the community already knew that her black cat Merlin was faring just fine, and she never mentioned having another.

Anyway, staying home and pouting in her corner was her loss, not mine.

And as far as losing went, dear Angelique was on quite a roll. On top of never getting Vazul, she received the kind of swift and brutal judgment anyone dreaded. Not only did Myrtil kick her out of her coven, but the Council declared that Angie would remain collared for an entire year and would be subjected to a three-year probation period. Should she stray again during that time, she would be permanently banned from using her powers. Her only hope then would be to flee the country. As covens communicated internationally, unless she found a rogue one to grant her asylum, anyone who found her would have her collared.

Although I was the injured party, I found the judgment a little excessive, especially since any actual damage had been averted. However, I understood that they were making an example out of her. As she had been such a prominent figure in our circle, it struck people all the harder that no one was immune from the Counsel's brutal discipline if they broke the rules. It had to be devastating for Angie to go from 'it girl' to complete pariah.

She eventually left town to start over where the stigma of her shame wouldn't rest so heavily on her shoulders. Unfortunately for her, word spread quickly, and she struggled to find a new home. Angie even tried to acquire a new Liderc egg, but no one would sell to her.

And it was a good thing, too.

Anger still burned in my gut every time I remembered the horrible plans she had in store for my demon had she succeeded in reclaiming him. There was no question in my mind that should she somehow manage to get a Liderc of her own, she would set that plan in motion, and maybe even push it farther. In fact, my gut told me that should such a dreadful day come, Angie would be extra abusive to her demon as retaliation for the humiliation and rejection she faced at Vazul's hand.

But she thankfully was no longer my problem. All I could say as far as she was concerned was good riddance to bad rubbish.

Meanwhile, I ended up joining Mrs. Hopkins coven. It blew my mind to discover what a wicked cool High Priestess she turned out to be. Behind that strict and excessively polished exterior hid the sweetest woman—so long as you walked straight.

To my chagrin, while she was willing to welcome Sophia into the fold, my friend respectfully declined. Like Angie, Sophia also craved power, even though she wanted to acquire it in an ethical fashion. A coven like the one led by Myrtil aligned better with her ambitions and the speed at which she could acquire said power.

Mrs. Hopkins catered more to green witches, those into practical and nurturing magic rather than those who sought brute power and offensive abilities. This totally met my own aspirations, and I quickly felt right at home within her coven. I was finally surrounded with like-minded people happy to offer support for the sake of camaraderie rather than as upfront payment in exchange for a favor later.

As for my demon, Vazul continued to bitch and moan about my efforts to make him my business partner. As I had previously promised myself, I wouldn't force his hand, but I would shamelessly continue to push him towards it. At least, he stopped complaining about me putting him officially on the payroll and giving him a very comfortable salary.

As much as he enjoyed having the funds to take me to all the human entertainment venues, he still struggled with the idea that I was the one paying his salary. It wasn't through some misplaced sense of misogyny. It just bothered him that he would technically be spoiling me with my own money.

"First of all, it's not *my* money, it's my *company* paying you," I said teasingly. "And if you were a partner, it would be *our* company's money. So…"

He made a face at me and muttered something unintelligible.

"Grumble and mumble all you want," I said in a taunting singsong voice. "Sooner or later, you know you will cave in. And if you don't, then so be it. Maybe I'll just have to ask that sexy accountant Frederick who seemed quite eager to help me grow my business."

Before I even finished my sentence, Vazul summoned one of his fiery tentacles, wrapped it around my waist, and yanked me to him with an angry look on his face. I chuckled shamelessly as I crashed against him. He held me with a possessiveness that had me tingling in all the right places even as he glared.

"If that wretch comes anywhere near you, I will drain him, reduce him to cinders, and use his ashes as decorative elements for your next miniatures. That shall be his contribution to helping grow your business," he hissed.

"You're so sexy when you're jealous," I purred, shamelessly batting my eyelashes at him.

"I do not share what's mine," he growled, his lips a hair's breadth from mine. "Maybe I should remind you why no partner will ever be better for you than me."

"Hmmm, maybe you should. With all the orders we had to fill lately, my memory of your non-crafting related skills is starting to get a little blurry," I said with a pout, my index finger tracing the areola of his right nipple.

The predatory smile that stretched his lips instantly had my stomach do a couple of backflips. He glanced to my right at a dresser we had been putting the finishing touches on. Full-scale furniture with embedded miniature elements had become our main business. The ones with interactive inserts or with magic-fueled animations were all the rage. And this one would be no exception.

"This dresser looks sturdy enough now. Maybe we should test it to make sure," Vazul said in a suggestive tone.

"Absolutely not!" I exclaimed, shocked. "No funny business on the merchandise!"

He scrunched his face and looked at me as if I was the biggest party pooper. "We've tested every other surface in the house already," he whined.

"Then get creative with new ways to use them," I said with a shrug. "After all, aren't Lidercs better sex demons than Incubi?"

"We are!" he said, sounding a bit offended.

"Then prove it!"

"Gladly!"

"Hold up! But not with anything funky this time. Let's see how good you can make vanilla," I said with a dare in my voice, expecting him to throw a fit.

To my shock, he narrowed his eyes at me, and a slow smile stretched his plush lips.

"Challenge accepted," Vazul said with a rumbling voice.

My demon picked me up and carried me like a bride instead of chest to chest with my arms and legs wrapped around him, like he normally did. A part of me felt cheated as we usually kissed all the way to wherever we would get down and dirty. Feeling his shaft hardening against my stomach as he carried me also was a cherished part of our foreplay. And yet, there was something possessive and romantic in the way he held me, almost like a treasured prize he was bringing back to his lair.

Except, I was already feeling too turned on to casually wait for us to reach our destination. I couldn't say when I became such a sex-starved maniac, but I wholeheartedly embraced that new me with my 'man.'

I leaned forward and brushed my lips over his neck, nibbling on it as my hand roamed over his tight abdominal muscles. His chest vibrated with a rumbling sound while his stomach contracted under my touch.

A part of me regretted issuing that challenge. It wasn't because I wished we would do one of those wild and unbridled scenarios he'd been delighting me with. I was in fact in the mood for something a bit more traditional, if that word made sense. But he would deem it as the signal that I wanted him to take over. Being naturally dominant, Vazul always tried to take control of our tumbles. But this time, I wanted to have my way with him a bit before relinquishing the reins.

I couldn't tell how many of those thoughts my demon was figuring out by reading my emotions. He couldn't read minds like that, but he could glimpse still pictures of things we humans conjured up in our heads, that we'd seen, or that we were focusing on. That was how he always knew exactly what my vision was for one of my pieces of furniture or miniature.

I peered at him, and his red eyes stared at me with an intensity that left me feeling bare. His face was unreadable but for a discreet smirk that seemed to promise both hell and paradise.

Vazul entered our bedroom and carefully placed me on the bed. I kicked off my shoes as he got onto the mattress and crawled over me. Before he was able to lay on top of me, I pushed his left shoulder, forcing him onto his back, then climbed on him.

"I want to do naughty things to you," I whispered, my palms resting on his shoulders, pinning him to the bed.

"By all means, Mistress. I'm yours to do with as you please... for now," he replied in a deep voice, the glow in his red eyes intensifying.

I had requested that he no longer refer to me that way as I didn't want our relationship to have that connotation of master and servant. Even though the magical bond between us technically set us as such, I believed in free will. We could establish our own rules, and ours was a partnership. Vazul was my boyfriend—and frankly the person I saw myself building a long-term life with—not my slave.

Although it initially struck him as strange, he honored my request when it came to regular interactions. But in the bedroom, every time I took the more dominant role, he would call me Mistress, like an obedient boy. And I loved it! In that instance, it was merely role play and consensual exchange of power. That was the type of dynamic I wanted between us.

"Good boy," I whispered with a triumphant smile.

I reclaimed his lips, my hands gliding over his bare chest. At home, Vazul always traipsed around naked but for a pair of shorts. In fact, he'd developed a predilection for kilts and mid-thigh-length Gothic man skirts. Obviously, with no undies underneath, as he was right this instant. The fiend shamelessly admitted that it sped up the process to see to my needs when I wanted a quickie.

As much as it had made my cheeks burn to be thus called out, I couldn't deny the accuracy of his claim. On a few occasions, I might have *forgotten* to wear undies of my own and *inadvertently* wiggled my behind while leaning over the island in the kitchen. A simple lift of our respective skirts had sufficed for a certain ridged snake to venture into an unassuming cave. My own wandering hands might have casually landed under the hem of his kilt and found themselves absent-mindedly playing jingle bells with his balls.

Even as our tongues mingled, I rubbed my palms over the chiseled grooves of his stomach. The fingers of my right hand ventured further down to his side to open the two buckle straps that kept it in place. Damn, how I loved the feel of his smooth skin, and the hardened nubs of his nipples beneath my touch!

I interrupted the kiss, feeling almost drunk on his sweet peach taste. Fisting his right horn, I tugged firmly to pull his head back. Vazul inhaled sharply, and the sound resonated directly between my thighs as my lips explored his face with devotion. His skin didn't quite possess the same texture as a human's. It was soft in some places, and slightly grittier in others, as if covered in the tiniest of scales. I couldn't quite put it into words, not that it mattered. I loved the feel of it against my lips and under my tongue.

He shivered when I began licking his neck, at that junction right below the ear, then nipped at his earlobe. Vazul growled his approval, and his fingers slipped through my hair to settle on my nape. I loved that he didn't attempt to control my actions, allowing me to explore his body as I saw fit. Obviously, it wouldn't last. He couldn't help eventually taking over. But I would savor what was mine for as long as I could.

I licked my way down to his chest, stopping for a brief moment so that my tongue could tease his nipples. Vazul moaned again, his abdominal muscles quivering in response to my ministrations. With a triumphant smile, I closed my lips around his little nub, slowly sucking on it. I flicked my thumb at the other, then pinched it hard enough that it would almost hurt. My demon liked a bit of pain. Once more, he grunted his approval. But it was the appearance of some fiery streaks under his skin that emboldened me.

While he could summon them at will, they often appeared involuntarily in response to pleasurable sensations. I immediately shifted my attention from his nipple to the streak running over his stomach. I traced it with my tongue, which tingled in reaction to the heat radiating from it.

As I licked the other streaks located further south, I opened the flaps of his kilt, revealing my prize. Finding Vazul already half erect awakened a dull throbbing between my thighs. Unable to resist, I made a beeline for it. Vazul hissed, his back partially straightening when my hand closed around his length. Fuck, my man was thick! It still blew my mind that I was able to take him.

And how glorious it was!

I marveled at the beauty of his shaft, with the swirling ridges that felt so wonderful inside me. They felt just as amazing against my palm as I began to stroke him. In seconds, a reddish glow appeared between the seam of the ridges, a telltale sign of my demon's pleasure. I leaned forward and gave his shaft a long, slow lick from the base to the head. Vazul hissed again, the sound turning into a growl when I took him deep in my mouth. He propped himself on his elbows to watch me swallowing him.

Vazul loved looking at his cock going inside of me, whether it be in my mouth or in my pussy. He hadn't been able to truly explain why. Yeah, it turned him on, but it was more than that. He explained that, in a way, it felt like each stroke further branded me as his, like a visual confirmation of our connection, which soothed his almost rabid possessiveness of me.

Whatever the reason, I didn't care. I loved having his cock inside me.

Tilting my head back, I peered up at him while making quite the spectacle of going down on him. I plastered the most lascivious expression on my face as I sucked on him, deepthroating as far as I could take, then gliding back up to the tip before swirling my tongue around the head. In between, I squeezed the base of his shaft, stroking it in counterpoint to the movement of my mouth, and fondled his balls just the way he liked.

It messed with my head that little ole me could give so much pleasure to a freaking thousand-some-odd-years old sex demon. And yet, there it was. My gaze locked with his, I reveled in the power I held over him. Eyes hooded, Vazul stared back at me with parted lips, his breathing growing increasingly louder and labored under my ministrations.

The strangled sound he emitted when I sank my nails between the seams of the ridges of his cock made me so damn wet, I felt it trickle down my inner thighs. Who would have thought pleasuring someone could be such an insane turn on? His moans in my ears, his hands fisting the blanket as he fought for control, the ridged texture of his shaft on my tongue, and his addictive peach cobbler taste in my mouth had my inner walls constricting with need.

I bobbed over him, one hand squeezing his testicles almost painfully, while my nails continued to stimulate the highly erogenous areas between the seams of his ridges. The sound of his rapturous moans, and the involuntary spasms in his legs heralded his imminent climax. I accelerated the pace, grazing his length with my teeth on each upward motion, and teasing him with my tongue as I took him deep in my throat.

As with all our previous encounters, I tried to convince myself that, this time, I'd get my man to completion this way. For a split second, when Vazul suddenly emitted a savage grunt, I actually believed he finally allowed himself to find his release first.

Buuuut nope.

The wretched male yanked my head back away from him. With lightning speed, my demon leaned forward, grabbed my waist, and all but body slammed me onto the mattress.

My stomach did a somersault in both fear and arousal when he lunged at me with an almost feral look on his face. Dazed, I barely realized how he managed to strip me out of my tank top and skirt. His hands and mouth were all over me, with an eagerness and passion that had every nerve ending standing to attention. He looked almost possessed as he kissed, caressed, and sucked on every inch of my body. Was I not seeing it with my own eyes, I'd think he had somehow summoned extra limbs to touch me with. And yet, he was managing this sensory overload with only one set of hands and his wicked mouth.

And the latter sure did a number on me.

An endless string of voluptuous moans tumbled out of me when Vazul buried his face between my legs. With him, you never knew if he would launch into a slow foreplay, teasing me with the most exquisite torture, or go straight for gold, making me sing arias right away. The question was instantly answered as his lips latched onto my little nub, sucking it with a frenzy while two of his fingers sank deep inside me.

My back arched off the bed as pleasure swiftly built in fiery waves. With deadly accuracy, my demon's expert touch stroked the sensitive spot inside me, sending lightning sparks throughout my body. Holding his horns with both hands, I gave myself over to him. My hips gyrated with a will of their own as he devoured me with relentless hunger. Legs trembling with my imminent climax, I chanted his name, spurring him on.

Although I saw it coming, my orgasm struck me with sweeping violence. I cried out, my body shaking as Vazul continued to feast on me for a while longer. Once I started coming back down, he relented and kissed his way back up my body. To my surprise, he didn't lie on top of me. Instead, he turned me onto my stomach and proceeded to worship every inch of me, the same way he had previously done for my front.

Naturally, he paid extra attention to my behind, which he absolutely adored. I loved when he opened his mouth wide and gave it a good chomp, as if he was trying to bite off a chunk. It never hurt, but I definitely felt it. And that half-pain always echoed back in my clit.

To my shock, he didn't give me a spanking. I loved the sting and the heated tingling that followed. But him raking his claws over my back, my butt, and behind my thighs wiped away all those thoughts. My legs shook violently in response, and my toes curled. I couldn't say why the lingering burning sensation was such a turn on for me, but it always had me throbbing in all the right places.

I gasped when he suddenly grabbed my hips and yanked my rump upward, propping me on my knees even as my face remained pressed on the mattress. A strangled cry escaped me when his mouth immediately settled on my pussy a second before his tongue speared into me. I fisted the blanket, my body shaking as Vazul stretched his tongue to impossible lengths, making it thicker as it thrust in and out of me.

With his claws continuing to set my skin ablaze and his

wicked tongue making love to me, my demon had me once more cresting in no time. My back seized as I cried out in bliss again. If not for Vazul keeping my behind propped up, I would have flattened on the bed.

Still flying high, I vaguely felt him pull his tongue out of me. Two of his fingers took over, this time rubbing my clit, keeping me riding that high. And then his thick cock poked at my opening. A bolt of lust exploded in the pit of my stomach as he pushed himself in. Between those first two orgasms and his fingers doing a number on me, Vazul had me so wet that my body welcomed him in quickly.

He never gave me a chance to fully recover before setting a frenzied pace. Good God! I would never tire of the insane sensation of his thick cock plowing into me. Between that and my clit getting frantically massaged, a series of micro-orgasms kept going off, taking me to the brink of madness. My demon fucked me hard, each friction of his ridges against my G-spot fanning the inferno that had liquid lava swirling in the pit of my stomach, then radiating throughout my nether region.

Vazul leaned forward, the intense heat of his chest over my back sending a violent shiver coursing down my spine. My skin erupted in goosebumps. His left arm slipped in front of me, pulling me up. His hand closed around my throat as he arched me back against him in a not fully kneeling position. I held onto his wrist, my other hand settling on the back of his, which was still rubbing my clit.

He pressed his lips to my ear as he continued to pound into me.

"Do you have any idea how much I love you?" he growled, sounding almost angry.

My heart leapt, and tears pricked my eyes from the powerful emotion his words elicited in me. I knew he had deep feelings for me, but I never expected such a confession, least of all so soon. I couldn't say I was there yet, but I was definitely headed that way with the speed of a freight train. However, I never had a chance to respond. A blinding light exploded before my eyes as I shouted, swept away by bliss.

The room spun as I tumbled down an endless vortex of ecstasy. Wave upon wave of pleasure crashed over me as my man continued to wreck me. Nothing else mattered but the searing heat of his body, in and around me, his lips and hands on me, and his cock destroying me.

It took me a moment to recognize the source of the red lights hovering overhead. I never felt when Vazul laid me down on my back. His delightful weight pinned me down on the mattress as he pounded into me with reckless abandon. He stared at me with glowing eyes, his face constricted by pleasure almost too intense, and his fangs bared.

Our voices mingled in blissful moans. I lifted my pelvis to meet him thrust for thrust, my nails digging into his back. My skin was on fire, and my nerve endings were ablaze. I was drowning in an ocean of pleasure as the slapping sound of our flesh meeting filled the room. My voluptuous moans and his feral growls intertwined in a sinful crescendo that would soon leave me shattered.

By the way he looked at me, touched me, made love to me, Vazul made me feel like the most desirable woman in the universe, and utterly cherished. In that instant, even as I neared the edge, I realized that I could never belong to another the way I belonged to my demon. He owned me, body, heart, and soul. I could die right here and now, consumed by the rabid passion he was unleashing on me.

And I wouldn't regret a thing.

My body seized as yet another orgasm crashed into me. I cried out with such violence, my throat hurt. Vazul roared, swept away as well when my inner walls clamped down on his cock. Had my brain not all but fractured, I would have been shocked that my lover hadn't slammed himself deep inside to fill me with his seed, as was usually his wont. Instead, a wild beast appeared to have taken over him as he went feral on me.

Vazul didn't relent. Even as his burning essence shot into me, he tightened his hold on my hips in an almost bruising fashion as he continued to fuck me hard. In my haggard state, I vaguely realized he had in fact managed to hold himself back, the spilling of his seed having stopped almost as quickly as it had begun.

Eyes closed, teeth clenched, he emitted the type of feral grunts you'd expect from a fiendish abomination from the deepest pits of hell. Something had broken inside of him. The beast was set free. It was too much, and yet somehow not enough. Each savage thrust of his brutal possession threatened to break me, casting me down into a maelstrom of pleasure and pain I would never emerge from. Fear and ecstasy warred within me in equal measure. I didn't want him to stop, even if it killed me.

I never saw my ultimate orgasm coming. I couldn't say whether I screamed or what other physiological response I had. It knocked my consciousness right out of my body. Vazul's shout resonated like thunderclap. But I was so far gone, it sounded almost as if I was hearing it underwater. His seed erupted inside me in burning, powerful spurts. With erratic movements, my demon kept rocking in and out of me until he was fully spent.

He collapsed on me before rolling onto his back. He drew me on top of him, holding me tightly as if he feared I would disappear. Boneless and utterly destroyed, I remained limp in his embrace, my head resting on his chest. The thundering sound of his heart slowly settling down acted like a beacon, guiding my consciousness back to my body.

"I didn't think you'd take my innocent challenge so literally," I slurred at long last.

He snorted then chuckled with a well-warranted smugness.

"Then you shouldn't have issued it, my Coral. I will always aim to exceed all your expectations and requests."

Still feeling a little groggy, I lifted my head to look at him. Instead of the arrogant expression I expected to find on his face, Vazul looked at me with a tenderness that made me melt from the inside out. At that moment, something settled in my heart.

"I think I'm falling in love with you, Vazul," I blurted out in a whispered voice, more to myself than for him.

The strangest expression flitted over his handsome features.

"No, my Coral. You *already are* in love with me. Your human brain needs more time to catch up, but your emotions do not lie," he said in a soft but factual voice. "It's okay, my beloved. Time is no longer a factor where you and I are concerned."

I should have called him out for being mightily presumptuous, but I knew his words to be true.

"Thank you for choosing me. Thank you for hatching for me. Thank you for making me the happiest woman in the world," I said instead.

"Now and always, my Coral. Now, and always."

THE END.

ALSO BY REGINE ABEL

THE VEREDIAN CHRONICLES
Escaping Fate
Blind Fate
Raising Amalia
Twist of Fate
Hands of Fate
Defying Fate
Imperial Fate

BRAXIANS
Anton's Grace
Ravik's Mercy
Krygor's Hope
Keran's Dawn

XIAN WARRIORS
Doom
Legion
Raven
Bane
Chaos
Varnog
Reaper
Wrath
Xenon
Nevrik
Rogue

PRIME MATING AGENCY
I Married A Lizardman
I Married A Naga

EMPATHS OF LYRIA
An Alien For Christmas

OTHER
True As Steel
Alien Awakening
Heart of Stone
Oops! I Summoned a Liderc

ABOUT REGINE

USA Today bestselling author Regine Abel is a fantasy, paranormal and sci-fi junkie. Anything with a bit of magic, a touch of the unusual, and a lot of romance will have her jumping for joy. She loves creating hot alien warriors and no-nonsense, kick-ass heroines that evolve in fantastic new worlds while embarking on action-packed adventures filled with mystery and the twists you never saw coming.

Before devoting herself as a full-time writer, Regine had surrendered to her other passions: music and video games! After a decade working as a Sound Engineer in movie dubbing and live concerts, Regine became a professional Game Designer and Creative Director, a career that has led her from her home in Canada to the US and various countries in Europe and Asia.

Facebook
https://www.facebook.com/regine.abel.author/

Website
https://regineabel.com

Regine's Rebels Reader Group

https://www.facebook.com/groups/ReginesRebels/

Newsletter

http://smarturl.it/RA_Newsletter

Goodreads

http://smarturl.it/RA_Goodreads

Bookbub

https://www.bookbub.com/profile/regine-abel

Amazon

http://smarturl.it/AuthorAMS